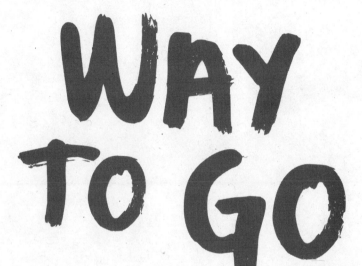

WAY TO GO

TOM RYAN

ORCA BOOK PUBLISHERS

Library and Archives Canada Cataloguing in Publication

Ryan, Tom, 1977-
Way to go / Tom Ryan.

Issued also in electronic formats.
ISBN 978-1-4598-0077-9

I. Title.
PS8635.Y359W39 2012   JC813'.6   C2011-907786-8

First published in the United States, 2012
Library of Congress Control Number: 2011943726

Summary: Danny is pretty sure he's gay,
but he spends his summer trying to prove otherwise.

*Orca Book Publishers is dedicated to preserving the environment and has printed
this book on paper certified by the Forest Stewardship Council®.*

Orca Book Publishers gratefully acknowledges the support for its publishing programs
provided by the following agencies: the Government of Canada through the Canada Book
Fund and the Canada Council for the Arts, and the Province of British Columbia
through the BC Arts Council and the Book Publishing Tax Credit.

Cover design by Teresa Bubela
Cover image by Getty Images
Author photo by Andrew Sargeant

ORCA BOOK PUBLISHERS   ORCA BOOK PUBLISHERS
PO Box 5626, Stn. B   PO Box 468
Victoria, BC Canada   Custer, WA USA
V8R 6S4   98240-0468

www.orcabook.com
Printed and bound in Canada.

15 14 13 12 • 4 3 2 1

For Andrew.
Things got better when I met you.

ONE

Kierce had a rule for every situation, and he never missed a chance to toss them at me and Jay like free candy. There were hundreds of them, but three were carved in stone.

Rule One: Keep a healthy mind in a healthy body. Kierce worked out every morning, and he tried to read at least one book a month. I could sort of understand the reading thing, but the thought of all that exercise made me sick to my stomach.

Rule Two: If you want to get rich, you've got to do well in school. Study as hard as you party. I was a good student, but I didn't see how that was going to help me get rich. I could tell you the years each of the provinces had joined Confederation, or the difference between mitosis and meiosis, but I wasn't actually *good* at anything. As for partying, well, let's just say that I wasn't the kind of guy who was known for holding his liquor.

Rule Three: Never, ever miss a chance to get laid. Kierce called this one the Golden Rule, and he spent a lot of time trying to follow it, with mixed results. I had a pretty good reason to ignore the Golden Rule completely, but I wasn't about to tell that to Kierce, or anyone else for that matter.

If I'd had rules of my own, they would have been more along the lines of, *Don't rock the boat*, or, *Keep your cards close to your chest.* My Golden Rule would have probably been, *When in doubt, get scared and clam up.* As for Jay, he wasn't really a "rules" kind of guy. Unless *No worries* counts as a rule.

Jay and I had been best friends since before we could talk. There's a picture of us side by side in our strollers, our moms standing behind us wearing hippie dresses, wooden beads and big sunglasses. Jay is beaming at the camera, and I look terrified. Typical.

The year we were twelve, he and I were sitting on his front steps when a moving van pulled in next door. Within five minutes, Kierce had strolled over and introduced himself to us as "the best thing to happen to Deep

Cove since sliced bread." It wasn't long before my dad was calling us the three amigos.

Until we were fourteen, we told each other everything. I knew that Jay had wet the bed until he was ten, and that Kierce's parents had gone through a rough patch before moving to Deep Cove. But when I woke up one night feeling horny and confused after a steamy dream about River Phoenix, I decided that some things were best kept to myself.

By the time I was seventeen, I had a lot of practice at keeping secrets.

ON THE LAST morning of exams, I sat in the school gym waiting for my grade eleven English final, the last thing standing between me and the summer of '94. I looked over at Kierce, who was turned sideways, balanced on the back two legs of his chair and flirting with Charlaine MacIntosh, who was doing her best to ignore him. Not that Kierce was the kind of guy to let that bother him. "Rule Seventy-three, Dan. If at first you don't get laid, try somebody else."

Three seats ahead of Kierce, at the front of the gym, Jay was tapping out a beat on his desk with a pencil. He looked pretty cheerful for a guy who hadn't handed in half of his assignments all semester. I doubted he'd even bothered to crack a book to study.

Finally the exam was passed out. I skimmed the questions and knew right away I wouldn't have any problems. I glanced at Jay. He was still smiling, but I could tell by the way he was squinting at the exam and slowly shaking his head that he was screwed. No big surprise, but it was still bad news. If Jay flunked English, he'd have to repeat the year, which meant he wouldn't graduate with us.

There was nothing I could do about it, so I turned back to the exam and got to work. After only half an hour, Jay got up from his desk and passed his exam to the teacher on duty.

After the exam, I met up with Kierce at our lockers.

"How'd you do?" I asked.

"Pretty good. I think I might have nailed the tough stuff, but who knows. Jay didn't stick around for too long."

"Yeah. Shit."

"Well, what are ya gonna do? Do you think he's at the Spot?"

"There's only one way to find out."

TO GET TO THE SPOT, you had to follow the abandoned train tracks for about a mile or so out of town, until you came to an old railway trestle that spanned a river gorge. If you scrambled down a slope that dropped from one corner of the bridge toward the river, and then hoisted yourself up onto a large cement anchor block underneath, you'd find yourself in a little room, hidden under the edge of the bridge with a clear view down through the trees and the brush to the river below. This was the Spot.

In the Spot, you felt as if you were both floating above the world and hidden beneath it. It was pretty comfortable—for a concrete slab—and ever since Jay and I had discovered it, a couple of years before Kierce came on the scene, it had been our regular hangout. Lately we'd been going to the Spot less frequently, but Jay still spent a lot of time there, even when Kierce and I weren't around. There were five kids in his family, and the Spot was the only place he could get some peace and quiet.

Sure enough, he was there, sitting cross-legged in the middle of the bridge, smoking. Kierce picked up a pebble and whipped it within inches of the cigarette.

Jay made a face of mock horror. "Hey! What's your problem?" he yelled.

"Rule Twenty-four: Smoking's for idiots! So, you finished that exam pretty early. Are you some kind of Shakespeare expert all of a sudden?"

Jay didn't answer. He just flicked his cigarette over the edge, stood up and threw his backpack over his shoulder.

"Let's get under," he said.

Kierce and I followed Jay under the bridge and up into the Spot. Once we were settled, he immediately lit up another smoke. Kierce pulled back and pretended to gag. "Jesus, Jay, you're gonna give us all cancer."

In answer, Jay edged a bit farther away and held the cigarette as far from us as possible. "All right, boys, I've got good news and I've got bad news," he said.

"I bet I can guess the bad news," I said.

He laughed. "Yep, I totally shit the bed on that exam. Guess I'll be sticking around this place for another year. Who knows, maybe I won't even bother finishing. Maybe I'll just head out west and make some real money."

Kierce rolled his eyes. "Don't be an idiot, man. Suck it up and finish high school, otherwise you're just asking for a miserable life."

"Maybe there's some way you can take extra credits," I said, "I don't know, summer school or something."

Jay looked at me as if I was insane. "Fuck summer school. I'm not gonna piss the summer away in a class-room, reading *Lord of the Flies* all over again."

"As if you read it the first time," said Kierce.

"Whatever. Some people just aren't cut out for school. Life's about more than books and tests."

"Yeah, it's about getting a hot girlfriend and buying expensive shit," said Kierce. "Good luck doing either without a high school diploma."

"We'll see," said Jay, his big smile plastered across his face as if he didn't have a care in the world.

Jay didn't seem to worry about his future at all, which amazed me. Sometimes I wished I could be that laid-back. I had good marks, but no more of a plan than he did. I certainly wasn't as motivated as Kierce, who wanted to be a lawyer. According to him, lawyers made piles of money and spent their free time cruising around on yachts with hot chicks.

"What's the good news?" I asked Jay. "You said you had bad news and good news."

"Are you kidding me?" he asked. He flicked his cigarette butt and watched it ricochet off a steel girder. "The good news is, school's out, losers! It's time to par-tay heart-tay."

"Speaking of summer, D-Man," Kierce said to me, "you gonna make it your mission to get laid before September, or what?"

"Yeah, I guess," I said.

I couldn't come out and say it, but I didn't care about getting laid. Over and over again, I'd tried to convince myself that I was going through a phase; that I just needed to meet the right girl; that as long as I didn't act on my feelings, or tell anyone about them, then my darkest fears might not be true.

I couldn't really be gay. Could I?

I imagined the whole town, led by Kierce, Jay and my family, chasing me out of town with flaming sticks and pitchforks, waving signs about *Eternal Damnation* and *Adam and Steve*. I just wanted to be normal, like everyone else.

I did my best to shove the problem to the back of my mind, hoping a solution would eventually reveal itself. That would have been a lot easier if Kierce wasn't so obsessed with my virginity. "Come on, guy," he said now, reaching out to punch me in the shoulder. "It's time to step up to the plate. Rule Sixty-two: Seize the day, dude."

"Yeah, I know. I'm doing the best I can," I said.

"I dunno, Danno," he went on. "You've gotta start making some moves. I mean, you're seventeen, for Christ's sake! Don't you want to experience the joys"— he clutched both hands over his heart, rolling his eyes upward and grinning like a moron—"of love?"

I gave him the finger. There was no point arguing with him.

"I'll tell you one thing," said Jay. "We've got two whole months with nothing to do but hang out, chase girls and go to the beach. Sounds like a pretty awesome plan to me."

It sounded like a plan to me too. At least, most of it did.

Two

On the first day of vacation, I woke up to the sound of my mom and sister moving around downstairs in the kitchen. I could smell bacon—a big deal in our house, where an exciting breakfast usually meant a choice between Cheerios and Rice Krispies.

"Look what the cat dragged in," Mom said as I walked into the kitchen. She smiled at me from across the kitchen island, where she seemed to be trying to cook something.

My sister, Alma, looked up briefly from her seat on the other side of the island, where she was flipping through *Leonard Maltin's Classic Movie Guide: 1992 Edition*. She dragged that book with her everywhere.

"All the gin joints in all the towns in all the world, and he walks into mine," she said.

Alma was thirteen and obsessed with classic films. She was always quoting stuff from movies nobody else had ever seen. Her room was plastered with pictures of old movie stars like Katharine Hepburn and Clark Gable. Even Orson Welles, chewing on a stogie, glowered down from over her bed.

"What's with the fancy breakfast?" I asked Mom. "Is something up?"

She smiled. "I was just thinking that since it's the first day of summer and all, I'd try to make a real breakfast for a change. Can't a mother do something nice for her kids?"

I sniffed the air. "Did you burn the bacon?"

Alma looked up from her book and rolled her eyes at me. "What do you think?"

My mom had lots of great qualities, but her cooking wasn't one of them.

"Bacon shmacon," Mom said, as she pulled the offending pan off the stove and covered it with a plate. "We've still got lots of eggs. How do you want them?" She stared down at a carton of eggs as if it had just dropped out of a UFO.

"This is great, Mom," I said, "but why don't you let me take care of it?"

"'You're a better man than I am, Gunga Din,'" said Alma.

Mom happily dropped onto a stool on the other side of the counter as I turned to rummage in the fridge. I managed to find a wrinkly green pepper, half an onion in a ziplock bag, and a rubbery chunk of bright orange cheddar cheese. I passed Alma the cheese and a grater, and started chopping up the veggies, stopping for a moment to heat up some butter in a banged-up old frying pan.

"Your dad called while you were out last night," Mom said.

"Oh, so that explains the good mood," I said, tossing the veggies into the pan and turning up the heat a little bit. "Were you guys using baby talk again?"

"It was gross," said Alma.

"Give me a break, you two," said Mom, barely able to keep the goofy grin off her face.

Four years earlier, the bottling plant in town had closed, putting my dad—and half of Deep Cove—out of work. A lot of families had left town after that, but my parents had chosen to stay in Cape Breton. Now, to make ends meet, my dad worked out west in the Alberta oil fields. Usually he was away for months at a time.

"He was sorry he missed you last night," she went on. "Next time he'll try to call when we're all here."

"Oh yeah, for sure. That'll be great." I quickly whisked up some eggs and added them to the pan, giving them a good shake and then adding the cheese Alma had grated. I turned the heat to low, covered the pan and, while I was waiting for it to cook, put some bread into the toaster.

I felt guilty about it, but I didn't really mind missing my dad's call. He and I were about as different as two people could be. He loved sports of all kinds, especially hockey, and I didn't have an athletic bone in my body. He loved hunting. I was afraid of guns. A tattered poster of Farrah Fawcett was pinned up over the tool bench in his garage. I kept Marky Mark's Calvin Klein ads hidden in the back of my *Royal Houses of Europe* encyclopedia. When you got down to it, there wasn't a hell of a lot for us to talk about.

Nothing, that is, except my future.

Dad may have given up on pushing me toward hunting and sports, but it had always been clear that he wasn't going to go as easy on me when it came to my plans for life after high school. Whenever I did end up on the phone with him, he'd start giving me suggestions about university programs or jobs he wanted me to consider. So far, I knew he'd be happy if I became a doctor, lawyer, engineer, investment banker or rocket scientist. It didn't matter that I wasn't interested in any of those careers. Besides, as he never failed to point out, it wasn't like I had any plans of my own.

I wished I *did* know what I wanted to do with my life—then I would have at least had something to talk to him about—but no such luck. It was easy to imagine living the high life in a big city like New York or London. It was a lot harder to figure out how I'd pay for any of it. I just couldn't get excited about anything, which frustrated the hell out of my dad. Missing his call meant one less opportunity to disappoint him.

I pulled the cover off the pan and cut the eggs into three pieces.

"*Voilà*," I said, throwing some toast on their plates and handing them across the counter.

"What is it?" asked Mom.

"It's a frittata," I said. "It's kind of like an omelet."

"'As god is my witness, I'll never be hungry again,'" said Alma, poking her fork dramatically into the air.

"I don't know where you learned to cook, Danny," my mom said, for probably the millionth time. "It sure wasn't from me."

It wasn't like it was some big secret or anything. With my dad away, and my mom working crazy hours,

I'd often ended up in charge of supper. You can only eat so many grilled cheese sandwiches, so I'd taught myself how to cook. I'd learned some things by reading my mom's rarely used copy of *The Joy of Cooking*, but most of it I'd picked up from watching cooking shows on TV when no one else was around.

After breakfast, Kierce and Jay came to pick me up in Kierce's mom's van. My family lived in the sticks, outside of Deep Cove, and since I didn't have my license, I had to rely on Kierce, my parents or my bike for transportation. It was a pain in the ass, and Kierce never let me hear the end of it, but I couldn't build up the nerve to take the driver's test.

We cruised into town and drove the strip for a while, wasting gas. If you believed my dad, Deep Cove had once been a boomtown, with a busy main drag full of shops and restaurants. Now it seemed like half of the businesses on Main Street were boarded up, and sometimes you had to wonder why there was a town here at all. In the summer we had the beach, but for the rest of the year, there wasn't much to do other than drive back and forth across town.

Kierce grabbed a tape from the glove box and shoved it into the stereo. He jacked it up and started rhyming along.

This is for the G'z, and this is for the hustlaz.
This is for the hustlaz, now back to the G'z.

Jay and I groaned. "Can't you give the rap shit a rest for five minutes?" asked Jay.

"You just don't appreciate the sounds of the street," said Kierce. "Probably because you guys have never lived in a city before." Kierce's dad was an RCMP officer, so his family had moved around a lot, which he claimed made him more worldly than us.

"Oh, right," said Jay, "the urban jungle of Saskatoon, where you picked up your *inna-city flava.*"

"Rule Ninety-nine," said Kierce. "Don't hate the *playa*, hate the game. Hey, what say we go grab some BS?"

"Now you're talking!" said Jay.

I shrugged. "Whatever, there's nothing else going on."

BS was the Burger Shack, a greasy spoon that the guys both loved. Personally, I thought the place was kind of gross. The decor hadn't changed since the seventies: the bright-orange walls were stained with decades worth of grease, and uncomfortable red metal chairs sat under rickety tables with chipped yellow laminate tops.

Worst of all was the food. Thin gray hamburger patties with rubbery fake cheese melted onto them, soggy fries, deep-fried zucchini sticks served with little packets of ranch dressing. Kierce and Jay couldn't get enough of the stuff, but every time we ate there, it made me want to try things I'd only read about or seen on TV: souvlaki with feta cheese and fresh tomatoes rolled up in pita bread, or hot crusty baguettes with Brie and thick slices of Italian ham. In Deep Cove, if you wanted to go out for dinner, the only choice was between the Burger Shack and a pizza place, which wasn't much better. At least the pizza place used real cheese.

The one good thing about the Burger Shack was its location, on the side of a hill between town and the beach. Whenever I looked out of its big grimy windows at the gently curving stretch of coastline, the tree-covered mountains that flanked it, and the moody sky moving endlessly over the sea, I could almost understand why my parents had chosen to stay in Deep Cove.

As Kierce pulled into the Burger Shack parking lot, we were surprised to find that it was empty. The blinds were drawn, and the place looked deserted. Jay pointed to a piece of loose-leaf stapled to the front door, and Kierce drove up close so we could read it. *BURGER SHACK IS CLOSED FOR BUSINESS.* In smaller letters underneath it read, *Re-opening soon under new management.*

"What the hell?" asked Jay.

"This totally sucks," said Kierce.

I didn't say anything. I'd get by just fine without greasy Burger Shack onion rings.

THREE

That night, Ferris Paulson threw a party. Ferris was on the hockey team with Kierce. He was kind of a jackass, but his parents were out of town and it was going to be a big party, so I wasn't about to miss it.

We picked up the beer Jay had scored for us and hidden at the Spot. Before heading to the party, we each downed one, and then cracked a road rocket. I hated the taste of beer, especially when it had been sitting outside in the heat all day, so I usually drank it in quick gulps to avoid the taste. By the time we got to the party, I was already kind of buzzed.

Ferris met us at the front door. "Come on in, boys!" he said, ushering us into the house. In the kitchen, a couple of girls were trying to point a speaker out the window so the music would blast into the backyard. Kierce beelined to them and started flirting, and I followed Jay out onto the deck so he could join the smokers. He lit a smoke, and we stood at the railing looking down at the crowd that had gathered around a bonfire in the backyard.

"Don't look now, Dan," said Jay, "but you've got an admirer."

He pointed, and I saw Michelle Donaldson waving up at me from the edge of the crowd.

"Oh shit," I muttered, giving her a halfhearted wave.

A year earlier, thanks to Kierce, who'd practically thrown me at her, Michelle and I had hooked up at a lame teen dance at the community center. Michelle was a year ahead of us in school and totally into me. It was horrible. We'd slow danced for a while, and then she'd practically dragged me into the woods to make out. It had been really awkward, but at least I'd finally made out with a girl.

I'd hoped things would end there, but I wasn't so lucky. For a few weeks, she did everything she could to get me alone, and we messed around a few more times. By messed around, I mean strictly above the neck; I wasn't going anywhere lower than her collar, and every time her hands had drifted toward my belt, I bolted like the Road Runner, leaving a little cloud of dust in my wake. Eventually, I'd just stopped returning her calls.

"What the hell, man?" Kierce had said. "You could've at least nailed her first!"

"Kierce, I'm not going to go out with somebody just to get laid."

He looked shocked. "Why the hell else would you go out with somebody?" Typical Kierce. He had a hard time accepting that his rules didn't apply to everyone.

Besides, I couldn't tell him that the only reason I *had* messed around with Michelle was because I felt like I was supposed to. After a while, Kierce had dropped it, but not before I heard a lot of rules about birds in hands and bushes, and striking with hot irons.

"Let's go down and check out the fire," said Jay, finishing his smoke and dropping the butt into an empty beer bottle.

"Do we have to?" I asked.

"You don't have to do anything you don't wanna do, my man," he said, slapping me on the back. "Maybe you should go see if *Wheel of Fortune* is on the tube."

"Fine," I said, "let's go."

Reluctantly, I followed him down to the backyard, where I opened another beer. I was starting to feel pretty good when all of sudden somebody tugged at my elbow from behind.

"Hey, you!" From the way Michelle was swaying, I could tell that she was even drunker than I was.

"Oh, hey, Michelle…"

She reached up and gave me a big hug, which she held a bit longer than necessary. Behind her back, Jay winked at me and then took off into the crowd, laughing.

"Yeah…hey, Michelle!" I repeated. "Congratulations on graduating. You still going to Toronto for university?"

"Yep."

Looking up at me with her goofy sideways grin, big sparkly eyes and rosy cheeks, she reminded me of one of Alma's old Cabbage Patch dolls. She held out her bottle of fruity wine and I took a swig, wishing for the millionth time that I could get away with drinking delicious girl booze instead of shitty warm beer.

"So, hey, great party, huh?" I said.

"Ummm…Danny, can I talk to you in private for a minute?"

"Uh, sure."

She grabbed me by the hand, and before I knew what was happening, she was pulling me toward a shed in the shadows at the back of the yard. Just before she dragged me behind it, I looked helplessly back at the crowd and saw Kierce grinning like a maniac and holding up three fingers. Rule Three: the Golden Rule. I wondered if he'd had anything to do with this. My back was up against the shed, and Michelle was standing uncomfortably close to me, still smiling her goofy smile. She smelled like booze and strawberries.

"I miss you, Danny."

I laughed awkwardly and downed the rest of my beer, then reached into my backpack to grab another one. "Hey, you want a beer?" I asked.

"No, I'm good." She held up her wine bottle. "Did you hear what I said?"

"Yeah, of course. I miss you too, Michelle…" I trailed off. What the hell was I supposed to say?

"Really?"

"Uh, sure."

"Because I'm moving away in a couple of months, and I've been thinking about—you know—unfinished business. Anyway, I know you're kind of shy, but maybe we just got off on the wrong foot."

She moved closer, wrapping her arms around my waist. Then she closed her eyes and stood on her toes, reaching up to kiss me. Instinctively, I reached out to hold her back, forgetting I had a beer in my hands. She squealed and jumped away as warm beer spilled onto her hair and down the back of her shirt.

"Shit, I'm so sorry!" I said.

"Oh my god! Did you do that on purpose?"

"Of course not!"

"What the hell, Danny? I can't believe you'd pour a drink over me to avoid messing around!"

I didn't know what to say, so I just stood there, my beer slowly sudsing over the top of the bottle.

"You know what, Danny? Maybe it's true what people say about you."

"What's that supposed to mean?"

"Well, it's not like there are all kinds of girls throwing themselves at you. It's just kind of weird that you don't seem interested."

"What are you talking about?"

"Forget it. Have a great summer, asshole!" She gave me a dirty look before heading back to the party. I wondered if I should follow her, but I was kind of reeling from what she'd said. What *exactly* did "what people say about you" mean? Suddenly Jay appeared around the corner of the shed.

"There you are. What the hell are you doing?" he asked.

"Oh, you know, just hangin' out behind the woodshed."

"You coming back to the party? Ferris just threw his folks' picnic table into the fire. He's pretty loaded."

"I know the feeling. I'll be out in a minute."

He pulled out a cigarette and lit up. "You okay?"

"Yep. Yepperoo."

He raised an eyebrow at me, but thankfully, he didn't pry. Above the noise of the party came the sound of angry yelling. Jay looked back around the corner of the shed. "Fight," he said. "Wanna go watch?"

"Hang on," I said. "I gotta lake a teak. Take a leak." I stood up, swaying.

"Shit, Danny, how much have you had to drink?"

"Oh, you know, four or five beers."

"We've only been here an hour!"

"I've still got a couple left."

"Well, slow down, or you'll end up puking."

"Yeah, yeah. Gimme a sec."

I took care of business, and we walked back over to the crowd that had gathered around what was now a full-fledged brawl. Ferris and some other goons were throwing haymakers at some guys I didn't recognize. Probably a hockey team from the next town over.

"This is awesome!" I said, and then yelled to nobody in particular, "GET THEM!"

Jay looked at me funny, and then Maisie Thomas ran up and poked Jay in the chest. "Guys are all the same. Fight, drink, screw. Soooo stupid!" She stopped and looked at me. "Oh hey, Danny. I wasn't talking about you. You're nice."

"Uh, thanks," I said. Maisie was in our class, but I didn't really know her very well.

"What's that supposed to mean?" asked Jay, laughing. "I'm nice too, aren't I?"

"Yeah, I guess," she said, "but you smoke cigarettes. I guess you think that makes you a badass or something."

"Nope," said Jay, flashing a big grin at her. "I just think it makes me look really sexy and cool."

"Whatever, Jay," she said, rolling her eyes but giggling at him anyway. She stumbled off into the crowd.

The fight wound down as quickly as it had begun, and I saw Ferris and one of the guys he'd just been fighting with give each other a man hug. The other guy asked Ferris, "Can I make some toast, dude?"

The excitement was over, and people got back to dancing around the fire. Kierce worked his way out of the crowd and over to us.

"Kierce!" I yelled. I raised my beer to greet him, but he wasn't smiling.

"Way to go, man," he said. "I just talked to Michelle. She basically told me that she wanted to get busy with you behind the shed, and you poured beer over her head and told her she was ugly!"

"That's not what happened!"

"Well, whatever happened, it sounds like you probably could have gotten laid, no strings attached, and you decided to run away, squealing like a little queer."

"Hey!" said Jay. "Take it easy, man!"

"You know what, Kierce?" I said, "It's none of your goddamn business. Besides, I don't remember you getting lucky recently."

"Yeah, well, the difference is, I try. I hate to break it to you, buddy, but people say shit about you, and I'm getting kind of sick of defending your ass. Rule Thirty-five: Turn down enough girls and people are going to stop suspecting that you're a fag and start assuming that you're a fag."

I glared at him for a moment, my mind spinning. There was nothing to say, so I turned and walked away from him, away from the party. Away from everything.

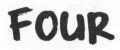

FOUR

I'd walked a few blocks by the time Jay caught up with me. "Kierce feels pretty bad, man."

I didn't look at him. "Whatever. I'm happy to know what people think about me."

"Dan, nobody thinks anything."

"Well, Michelle thinks I'm queer. And so does Kierce, apparently!" I turned to him. "Do you?"

I wanted him to tell me that he didn't care either way. That being gay was no big deal. Instead he said, "Of course I don't. But you know what girls are like. They talk about everything. You turn a couple of them down, and they start thinking you're weird. But who cares?

I know you, and you know you, and that's all that matters, right?"

"Yeah."

"Besides," he went on, "what do you care what people say about you?"

Easy for him to say. Jay had no problem sliding through life with his big old grin. He hadn't grown up wondering what was wrong with him, terrified that if people knew the truth, he'd be mocked and beat up, hated by everyone. I didn't answer him.

"Do you want to go back to the party?" he asked.

"No way."

"Me neither. Let's go back to my place. We'll grab something to eat and play Super Metroid."

We walked on in silence, taking shortcuts through backyards and weed-filled empty lots. When we were a few blocks from his house, Jay ducked behind a building to pee. I pulled a beer out of my bag and cracked it, then strolled around the corner to wait for him. I was mid-chug when the colored lights of a cop car flashed on.

Instead of running, I froze, and before I knew it, Kierce's dad, Officer LaVoie, was getting out and walking over to me. Jay was nowhere to be seen. I hoped he'd seen the lights and taken off in the other direction.

Kierce's dad shone his flashlight at my beer and then up into my face. I could tell by the way his eyes widened that he was surprised to see me. He put his hand on my back and directed me over to the car.

"Why don't you go ahead and open up your bag, Danny," he said.

Reluctantly, I unzipped it, revealing my one remaining can of beer. He opened the back door to the car and told me to get in.

I sank miserably into the backseat. Officer LaVoie ignored me, shuffling through papers for what seemed like an eternity. Finally, he turned around to face me.

"So, Danny, you out for a bit of fun tonight?"

"Yeah. I guess."

"The beer's yours?"

"Yeah."

"Okay, that's what I figured." He made a quick call on his radio, but he spoke in some kind of cop code, and I couldn't understand what he was saying.

"So here's what we're gonna do," he said when the call was over. "I have to give you a fine for underage drinking."

I dropped my head and managed to stifle a depressed belch.

"You're seventeen?"

I nodded.

"Okay, that means I won't have to call and wake up your parents. You're old enough to deal with this yourself." He took a few minutes to fill out a carbon-paper form, then he ripped off the pink copy and handed it through the grill to me. "Now, you want a ride home?"

I couldn't tell him that I was staying at Jay's house, in case he waited around for Jay to show up, so I agreed.

He let me out of the backseat so I could sit up front, and then he drove me all the way to my house and dropped me off at the foot of my driveway.

"I'm gonna make a suggestion, Dan," he said as I was getting out of the car. "If I were you, I'd come clean with your folks. It'll probably save you a bunch of bullshit down the road."

THE NEXT MORNING, I woke up with a pounding headache. After a couple of foggy moments, I began to remember the night before. I lay in bed for a few minutes, considering Kierce's dad's advice. I decided he was right and dragged my ass downstairs to face the music.

Mom listened to the whole story—minus the part about what Kierce had said to me—and then sighed. "Danny, I really don't have time to worry about this stuff right now."

"You don't have to worry, seriously!"

"Oh really?" she said. "You get picked up by the cops for underage drinking, and I'm not supposed to worry?"

"It's true, Danny," said Alma. "Hooch is dangerous. One minute you're enjoying a refreshing gimlet with your chums, and the next you're lying facedown in a ditch with puke all over your fedora. Haven't you seen *Days of Wine and Roses*?"

"Where did you *come* from?" I asked her.

"Alma, sweetie, why don't you go up to your room so I can talk to Danny privately," said Mom.

"'Story of my life,'" Alma said. "'I always get the fuzzy end of the lollipop.'" She clomped up the stairs.

Mom poured herself a cup of tea and sat down at the table across from me.

"So what are we going to do about this?" she asked me.

"I don't know. Ground me, I guess?"

"I might have a better idea."

"What do you mean?"

"Your dad has been suggesting for a while that it's time you got a job. I didn't think it was necessary, but now I'm starting to think it's a good idea."

Typical of my old man to decide what was best for me without my input.

"A job?" I asked. I'd always figured I'd get one after high school to help pay for university or whatever,

31

but it had never occurred to me that I should get one any sooner. It wasn't like Deep Cove was crawling with jobs.

She went on. "I don't like the idea of you bumming around town all summer, getting into trouble just because there isn't anything better to do. Anyway, it turns out that I might have a lead for you."

"What do you mean, a lead?" I asked skeptically.

"You know the Burger Shack?" she asked.

"It's closed!"

"I know that, but it's not going to stay closed for long; it's just not going to be the Burger Shack anymore. I ran into an old high school classmate of mine the other day, Denise Turner. She's back in town, and she's bought the building. She plans on turning it into a restaurant."

"It's already a restaurant."

"I mean a real restaurant, with tables and chairs and a patio. With an actual menu. Not just burgers and fries. Anyway, she's cleaning the place out, and she's looking for some help so she can open as soon as possible."

"I don't know," I said. "What kind of stuff would I be doing?"

"First you'd be helping get the place ready, but she told me that she'd be willing to hire you on after that to help out. Maybe you'll wait tables, or help in the kitchen, who knows? You'll learn a lot. Denise has worked in some great restaurants. What do you think?"

"I guess so," I said. It didn't sound like a great idea to me, but I wasn't really in a position to argue.

"Hey, it's not the end of the world. Your father and I both had jobs in high school. Don't you think it could be kind of fun to do something different for the summer?"

"Yeah. Sure. I guess."

"Well, I'll give Denise a call in a while, and if it still sounds good to her, I'll drive you down there to meet her this week."

"Okay," I said miserably, imagining the reaction I'd get from the guys.

"Danny," she said, "I know you think this is going to wreck your summer, but honestly, some of my best memories come from when I used to wait tables. This could turn out to be a great experience."

I nodded, trying not to look too upset. It was hard to look on the bright side when the long lazy summer I'd been looking forward to had just disappeared.

I called Jay from my room.

"What the hell happened last night?" he asked.

"What do you think happened? Did you see the cop car?"

"Yeah, I noticed the lights, so I got the hell out of there. I waited outside in the yard for almost an hour, but when you didn't come back, I figured you must have been busted."

"Yep."

"Did you tell your mom?" he asked.

"Yeah, and get this. I have to get a job."

"What? No way!" he said.

"Way."

"Hang on a second," he said. I heard muffled voices, and all of a sudden Kierce—the last person I wanted to talk to—was on the line.

"Hey, buddy," he said.

"Hey."

"I can't believe my dad busted you. That totally sucks!"

"Yeah. At least he gave me a ride home."

"Listen, D-Man, I'm really sorry about last night. I shouldn't have said that shit. It's none of my business if you don't want to mess around with Michelle."

"S'all right."

"Seriously! I didn't mean to be such an asshole. I was just looking out for you, dude. Some guys in the locker room said some shit a couple of times. You know what hockey players are like. They think you're some kind of fag if you aren't banging a new girl every week.

34

Anyway, I stood up for you, man, 'cause I know you aren't a fag. I just want you to get some action once in a while, Dan! Are we cool?"

My stomach flipped every time he said *fag*, but all I said was, "Yeah, we're cool."

"Sweet, man. Anyway, my old man is totally breathing down my neck. He won't believe me when I tell him I wasn't drinking with you last night. That's kind of the funniest part of the whole thing."

"What is?" I asked.

"In a million years, who'd have thought *you'd* ever be considered a bad influence?"

After I hung up, I lay on my bed and stared at the wall. I'd been listening to people shoot their mouths off about fags and queers and fruits since we were kids. That kind of stupid jock talk was as normal as someone asking you to pass the salt. But this was different. This was personal.

I'd always thought I was doing a pretty good job of flying under the radar. Apparently not. Kierce might have been a total asshole at the party, but he was right about one thing. I needed to put the rumors to rest.

FIVE

A couple of days later, as we drove to the restaurant to meet Denise, my mom told me a bit about my new boss.

"She was a lot of fun, kind of a bad influence. She was always getting us to skip class and do crazy stuff. We thought we were a bunch of rebels." She laughed, as if remembering something funny.

I glanced over and tried to imagine my mom as a rebel. I pictured her with a mohawk and a leather jacket instead of a perm and a quilted vest and turtleneck. It was hilarious to think about, but not very believable.

"Why have I never met her?" I asked.

"Well, she's been gone for a long time, since right after high school. She didn't get along very well with her parents, and I don't think Deep Cove was big enough for her."

"How come?"

"Not everyone can stand living in a small town. There's a lot of gossip, and not many opportunities."

"Tell me about it."

She gave me a funny look but didn't say anything else as we pulled into the parking lot of what had been the Burger Shack. She parked next to a pickup truck piled high with old tables, chairs and other junk from the restaurant. The Burger Shack sign—an orange and purple monstrosity with a dancing hamburger painted on it— sat broken in two on top of the heap of garbage.

The front door was locked, but we could hear some kind of commotion inside, so we walked around to the back of the building. A tall thin man who looked to be in his forties was leaning against the wall smoking a cigarette.

"'Ow's it going?" he asked in a thick French accent.

"Very well, thanks," my mom replied. "Is Denise around?"

"Denise is in the back, in the kitchen. If you wanna call it that."

We headed inside. The place was a mess, and the only thing that indicated it had ever been the Burger Shack was the orange paint on the walls. From behind the swinging door that led to the kitchen, we heard a loud crash.

"Shit!" somebody yelled. I followed my mom through the door and toward the voice.

The kitchen was a lot cleaner than the dining room, but it still looked like a tornado had hit it. Large kitchen appliances, still wrapped in plastic, stood next to a pile of open cardboard boxes that appeared to be full of plain white dishes. Standing in the middle of the chaos was a stocky woman with curly brown hair held down by a Red Sox cap. She was wearing a pair of jeans and a ratty old T-shirt that said *Kiss the Cook*. She looked up and marched over to us as we came in.

"Good to see ya, Mary," she said, reaching over to give my mom a quick hug and slapping her on the back. She turned to me. "You must be Danny. I'm Denise." She held out her hand and almost crushed mine when we shook.

"Hi," I said.

"So your old lady here tells me that you're up for a bit of a challenge, eh?"

"Yeah, I guess so."

"Well, you can start by cleaning out the toilets. There should be a toothbrush on one of the sinks back there."

I stayed where I was and glanced at Mom, shocked. Toilet? With a toothbrush? Denise let out a huge burst of cackling laughter and slapped me on the back. Hard. "I'm just busting your balls, my man!"

My mom also seemed to find it really funny. I shot her a dirty look as she left.

"So here's the deal," Denise told me as she led me back into the dining room. "I want to open this place as soon as we can get all our shit together, which is gonna mean a lot of long days between now and then. Are you up for it?"

I nodded. "Yeah, for sure."

"Good stuff. First order of business is to get the kitchen organized, and then we're gonna clean and paint the rest of the place from top to bottom. When we're through, I want it to look like a totally new restaurant."

I looked around and took in the piles of garbage scattered around the room, the grimy windows, the filthy floor. I must have looked skeptical.

"Don't worry, Dan," she said. "We'll just have to do our best and hope that's good enough."

The guy who'd been smoking when we came in was Jean Pierre, who told me he preferred JP. He was a friend of Denise's from Montreal, and despite his grubby appearance, he was a classically trained chef.

"Denise knows that I wouldn't come to the middle of nowhere for anyone else in the world," he said as he stood back and directed us as we dragged shelving units around the kitchen. "Especially with what she's paying me!"

"Quit your bitchin', old man," she said. "This is the first vacation you've had in ten years."

"Vacation? Ha! Slaving over a hot stove in some godforsaken town with the worst wine selection east of Montreal is not a vacation," he said. "And she's too cheap to hire me a sous chef!"

"What's a sous chef?" I asked.

"A sous chef is the person who does all the kitchen work while the chef stands around feeling very important," said Denise.

"A sous chef," said JP, ignoring her, "is a chef's assistant. His second-in-command. A sous chef helps with prep work, salads, desserts. Anything the chef needs. A very important position; too bad Denise doesn't see it that way. The woman will be the death of me, mark my words."

We dragged the final shelf into place, and he stood in the middle of the kitchen with one hand on his hip and the other one scratching his chin, slowly moving in a circle, checking it all out.

"This will do for now," he said. "It's not perfect, but it will do."

Denise told me that after she left Deep Cove, she waited tables for a long time before eventually working her way up to restaurant manager. She'd lived and worked in lots of different cities, including Montreal, where she'd met JP, and New York, which she assured me was as extraordinary as I imagined.

"Restaurant work can be a real pain in the ass," she said, "but some people are born for it, and I guess I'm one of them."

"What made you decide to open your own place?" I asked her as we unpacked boxes full of bowls and mixers and bizarre utensils.

"When my mom died last year," she told me, "I came home to take care of her things, and believe it or not, I realized that I actually missed Deep Cove."

"Really?" I asked. If you'd lived in New York or Montreal, wouldn't Deep Cove be about the last place you would want to live?

"Yeah, it definitely surprised the shit out of me," she said, "but when you get a bit older, you see things differently. Anyway, I heard the Burger Shack building was for sale, so I pulled together my savings and bought the place. My friends all told me they were worried I was making the decision too quickly."

"No, we said you were crazy," JP said without looking up.

"Yeah, well, you came with me, monsieur, so who's crazier? The crazy woman, or the man who follows her?"

JP just grunted and went back to arranging cookbooks on the shelf above his workspace.

"Anyway," she went on, "sometimes you just have to go with your gut. I was looking for a change, and this seemed like the right thing to do. Opening a restaurant isn't easy though. If JP wasn't here, I don't know how I'd keep it all together."

"So when we open, will I be waiting tables?" I asked.

I heard JP chuckle across the kitchen, and Denise smiled and shook her head.

"I hate to break it to you, buddy, but I'm gonna need you in the kitchen. You, my friend, are going to be occupying one of the most important positions in any restaurant, the heart and soul of any successful operation." She looked up and smirked at JP. "You're going to be the head dishwasher."

It wasn't my dream job—I had no idea what that was yet—but I figured that I had to start somewhere. Denise told me that once the place was open, I'd have more time off, but until then, I was going to be busy all the time. It didn't bother me. I was making money and learning a lot about the business from watching Denise and JP.

Having no free time was also a good excuse to avoid Kierce. I was still pretty pissed off at him, and ever since the party, I couldn't stop wondering whether everyone else in Deep Cove thought I was gay.

It was so confusing. Being gay was the last thing on earth that I wanted, but my body refused to cooperate with my brain. I had to figure something out. I wasn't religious, so "praying the gay away" wasn't going to work, but I'd heard about places that claimed to be able to fix someone like me—make me "not gay." From the little I knew of these camps and clinics, they were expensive, and most of them were in the southern States. How would I explain that to my parents? *Hey, Mom and Dad, I think I have the hots for Johnny Depp. Can you give me five thousand bucks so I can go to Camp Homobegone in Alabama?*

The simplest, most obvious solution was something I could do on my own. I needed to find a hot girl and get *her* to help me change. This was much easier said than done. In my head, I ran through a list of all the single girls I knew.

Michelle Donaldson. Obviously out of the question.

Anna Hobbes. Too wispy.

Diana Grant. Too breasty.

Charlaine MacIntosh. Too aggressive.

Maisie Thomas. Too giggly.

I ruled out one girl after another. I'd known all of them for most of my life, and I'd literally never had one sexual thought about any of them. I was not off to a good start. I knew what I had to do, but I was missing the right girl to help me do it. So to speak.

SIX

A few days after I started working, my mom dropped me off early at the restaurant. I was the only one there, since Denise and JP were out of town picking up a truckload of tables and chairs. The night before, Denise had given me a key and asked me to paint the trim in the dining room.

I started a pot of coffee. While I waited for it to brew, I examined the intriguing array of supplies that JP had carefully unpacked from a stack of sturdy plastic containers and arranged neatly on a large shelving unit at the back of the kitchen. Denise had made it clear to me that I shouldn't touch anything on those shelves.

"That's JP's pantry stock from Montreal. He'll slice your fingers off if you mess with his system."

I decided that what JP didn't know wouldn't hurt him, and I rooted around in his supplies, being careful to put things back exactly as I'd found them. Some of it was familiar to me—bags of rice and boxes of pasta, large cans of tomatoes from Italy, jars of black olives.

A lot of things, though, I'd never heard of. Inside a battered old tin box, I found several bags stuffed with dried peppers of different sizes and colors. There were thick tubes of yellow paste called polenta, and little bottles of coriander, saffron, tarragon and garam masala. I examined jars full of marinated artichoke hearts and pickled capers. I unscrewed a tiny bottle of white truffle oil and sniffed; it was like nothing I'd ever smelled, pungent and sweet. I wondered what you used it for and why the bottle was so small.

The coffee stopped dripping. As I poured myself a cup, I heard a vehicle pull into the parking lot on the other side of the building. I walked back through the dining room to look out the window and saw that an old beater of a hatchback had pulled up near the front door. Someone was bent over, rummaging around in the backseat.

A girl stood up, holding a huge quilted cloth bag, and slammed the car door shut. She was almost my height, with a long wavy mass of reddish-brown hair that was held back with an elastic. As she swayed up to the front door, I ducked back from the window, trying to act casual as she walked into the restaurant.

She was beautiful. Tall and willowy with pale, lightly freckled skin. She was wearing cut-off jeans and sandals with leather straps that were tied up past her ankles. A lacy shirt, embroidered with flowers, was knotted over a green tank top. I saw the edge of a tattoo— it looked like a green rose—peeking up from behind the back collar of her shirt. Dozens of bangles jingled on her wrist, and her fingers flashed with big gaudy rings. She looked to be around my age, but nothing about her was familiar. She was clearly unlike any of the girls I knew from Deep Cove. She took a quick look around and then turned to me, her shimmering pale-green eyes staring right into mine.

"This is the place, huh?" she asked.

"Yeah, I guess so."

"Who are you?"

"I'm Danny. I work here, with Denise. For Denise."

"What a coincidence. So do I."

She walked over to the counter and dropped her bag, then wandered into the kitchen. I followed her and watched as she poured herself a coffee.

"Denise told me that this place was kind of grubby," she said, looking around. "No shit. So what are we supposed to be doing today anyway?"

I didn't understand; Denise hadn't mentioned anything about some strange girl showing up to work. "I'm supposed to paint the trim in the dining room," I told her.

"Painting. Okay, I can help with that."

I must have looked confused, because she laughed and said, "You're wondering who the hell I am, and why I'm here."

I nodded.

"Fair enough. I'm in town for the summer to stay with my aunt, who is friends with Denise. Denise asked me if I was interested in waiting tables for the summer, and since I don't know anybody around here, I figured, what the hell. I've waited tables in much fancier places than this, so it's no big deal."

She tipped her coffee into the sink and then did the same with what was in the pot. "You make really shitty coffee," she said as she set about brewing some more. "I was called out of town because there was a bit of an... issue...with my mom. It's, well, it's basically the same reason I'm here for the summer in the first place." She shook her head, as if to dislodge a thought. "Long story.

Anyway, I ended up coming back earlier than expected, and I figured I'd stop by to give Denise a hand."

"Where's home?"

"Home? Home is where the heart is, right?" She laughed, and I just smiled back, trying to figure out how to respond to her. "I live in New York."

"City? That's cool."

"Yep, the Big Apple. Not that cool, though, unless you like bums and businessmen. Give me your cup. I won't let you drink that swill."

On a map, New York wasn't really all that far away from Deep Cove, but she might as well have told me she lived on Mars. It explained a lot. Her confidence, the way she talked, her clothes…

She handed me a fresh cup of coffee with a flourish. "Now, if you don't have any more questions, let's go paint some trim!"

"I have one more question…"

"Shoot."

"Ummm…what's your name?"

She struck a pose, turning sideways and holding an imaginary pistol up to her face. "Lisa. Lisa Walsh," she said, blowing make-believe smoke from the barrel.

For three awesome hours, Lisa Walsh and I talked and painted and listened to music. Well, mostly I did the painting and she did the talking, but she had more than enough to say for the two of us. She had all kinds of stories, like the time in ninth grade that she and some friends had snuck out at night to try and see Nirvana at a club in Brooklyn.

"We didn't even make it past the security guard," she said, "but we could hear them from the alley. It was pretty rad." Her big cloth bag held an astonishing array of random crap. When she pulled out a pair of old cutoffs and a ratty Guns N' Roses T-shirt for painting, I caught a glimpse of a big old camera and a deck of cards. After she'd changed in the bathroom, she unearthed a thin purple package of super-skinny black cigarettes. "I don't usually smoke," she said, standing in the doorway and lighting up, "but these are French, and sometimes I just want to be like *that*, you know?" I nodded, although I had no idea what she was talking about.

When she was done smoking, she pulled an assortment of mix tapes out of the bag and tossed them on the floor. They all had unique handmade covers: carefully glued collages of magazine images and hand-drawn cartoons, with the names of the songs handwritten on the insides in intricate lettering.

"My friends and I have a tape swap. Every few months each of us puts together a mix tape and makes a bunch of copies to pass around." She dragged JP's busted-up old double cassette player into the center of the room and shoved a tape into it, fast-forwarding to find the right song. While I painted, Lisa played DJ on what she dubbed *le boom box*. Every song seemed to have a story.

"Okay, hang on," she said, her finger paused over the Play button. "So this one is my friend Naomi's favorite. She totally lost her virginity to this guy last year, some creepy painter dude who hung out at her mom's gallery. He was super old, like twenty-five or something, but she totally dug him, and before they did it, she made him wait so she could put this song on. Naomi's a total drama queen. She'll be famous for sure." She pressed *Play* and the room filled with a smoky voice singing jazz. I couldn't tell if the singer was male or female.

> *Just in time, you've found me. Just in time.*
> *Before you came, my time was running*
> *loooooooowwwwww...*

"Wow," I said. "I've never heard anything like that."

"You like it? Nina Simone. She's amazing. She's like the most badass ever." Lisa dropped to the floor and twisted her legs into a yoga pose, and then, just as quickly, she bounced back up and twirled around the room.

I was getting used to the random movement; she seemed unable to sit still.

"New York now is so clean and perfect," she said. "It's not edgy at all anymore. Back in the day, like in the fifties and sixties, you could get all slicked up in dresses and suits and go sit in smoky clubs and drink martinis and hear Nina or listen to Beat poets. Man, that must have been so—I don't know—authentic, you know what I mean? Now it's just so lame."

I didn't really get half of her references, but it seemed to me that New York was just about the opposite of lame, especially compared to Deep Cove. Lisa rummaged around for another tape. "Okay, check this one out!" She pressed *Play* and the room was filled with shimmery hypnotic notes that were gradually joined by thumping drums and bass. She started to dance around the room, slithering over to where I was standing and grabbing me by the hands, pulling me toward her.

"Come on, dance!"

I was a terrible dancer, the worst. And on the rare occasions that I'd danced in the past, it had at least been to music I knew. This music was bizarre, endlessly repeating itself while somehow creating something new. I resisted, but she grabbed my arm and pulled me around the room, and eventually I found myself moving with her, with the music, letting it slide my limbs into the right places, letting the sounds do the thinking for me.

When the music died away, we stood there exhausted and laughing.

"Embarrassing," I said.

"Why? Dancing is everything!" She flopped into a cross-legged yoga pose on the floor next to her bag and looked up at me. "Don't you dance?"

"No. At least not like that. I don't think I've ever heard music like that."

She laughed. "That's Underworld. Rave music."

"Rave?"

She looked at me with disbelief.

"You're kidding me," she said. "*You*, my friend, have a *lot* to learn."

Our party was interrupted by the sound of Denise's truck pulling up to the building. Doors slammed, and Denise came into the dining room.

"Lisa! You made it!"

Lisa jumped up and ran over to give Denise a big hug.

"I hope you haven't been corrupting little Danny with your evil big-city ways," Denise said.

"Mister Dan has been a perfect gentleman."

Denise took a look around the room. "The trim looks good, Dan. Can you go out and help JP unload the tables from the truck?"

On my way out the door, I heard Denise, her voice low and serious, ask, "So how's your mom doing?"

That night, I had a hard time getting to sleep. I couldn't stop thinking about Lisa. She wasn't like any girl I'd ever met. I imagined the two of us traveling around the world together, lounging on oceanside patios in elegant clothes, toasting each other with well-iced cocktails. Was this what having a girlfriend could be like?

Maybe Lisa had appeared out of nowhere for a reason. I was kind of like a frog in a fairytale who needed a kiss from a princess so he could turn into a prince. Only, instead of a frog, I was a might-be-gay kid who needed straightening out, and instead of a princess, she was a cigarette-smoking tattooed city girl with a bagful of mix tapes. I figured that was close enough.

SEVEN

Over the next few days, the four of us worked like crazy to get the restaurant ready for opening day. We finished painting the whole place, and we installed new light fixtures in the dining room. Flowers were planted around the outside of the building, the floors scrubbed until the original color of the tiles came through. Just as my mom had predicted, I loved my job.

Best of all, Lisa and I were really connecting. She told me stories about New York and the amazing things she'd seen and done there. She'd been on family trips to San Francisco and Paris and even Tokyo. She'd done so many things that I'd only dreamed about. We were the same age, but it seemed to me she had a big head start in life.

I couldn't tell if she thought of me as boyfriend material though, or if she just wanted to be friends. She was always throwing her arms around me and giving me spontaneous hugs, or reaching out to mess up my hair. She spent so much time talking or laughing or dancing that it was hard to tell what she was thinking most of the time. Every once in a while, she'd get kind of moody and stop talking altogether, but it never lasted long. With Lisa, you learned to just go with the flow.

The main thing was that she seemed to like me, which was a good start. Now I had to figure out how to get her to *like me* like me. As in, want to jump my bones and make a man out of me. If I could make that happen, it would prove to everyone—and to me—that I wasn't gay.

If only it was that simple. I couldn't really figure out how I felt about her. I thought she was totally beautiful, not to mention the most interesting person I'd ever met. But even though I thought about her all the time, I didn't care about what she looked like naked. I never thought about having sex with her. I just wanted to be around her all the time.

On the night before the opening, we ended up working till well after dark putting the finishing touches on the place. It was almost midnight when Denise told Lisa and me to stand back and look at the dining room.

"What do you guys think?" Denise asked.

"I think it looks great," I said, and Lisa agreed. The walls were painted a soft bluish gray, the color of the ocean in the morning, and the tables were set with crisp white linens. On top of each one was a small vase of wildflowers, and on the walls were photos Denise had taken of the local area. Fishing boats heading in from the catch, kids playing on the beach, wild rose bushes beside a dusty dirt road. It looked like a real restaurant. Denise couldn't stop smiling.

We joined JP in the kitchen, where he was putting the finishing touches on his workspace. The stainless steel gleamed, the shelves were neatly stocked and the big glass-fronted refrigerators were full of food.

"Hey, JP, if you're not too busy admiring your reflection in the counter, why don't you whip us up something to eat?" Denise said.

"Denise, Denise, when the clock strikes ten, I turn into a little pumpkin. You know that."

"What if I grab us a bottle of wine from out front?"

"Now you're talking. How about you kids? Are you hungry?"

We nodded, and he motioned to us to pull up some stools around the counter.

"If you wanna eat my food, you gotta watch me make it. Look and learn, friends. You'll be happy you did. But first, some music, don't you think?"

He dug around in a stack of tapes on the shelf next to *le boom box* and snapped one on. The kitchen was filled with music that made me feel like dancing, and that's exactly what JP did, shimmying around the kitchen, grabbing veggies and a knife, and chopping with lightning speed.

Then that time I went and said goodbye,
Now I'm back and not ashamed to cry,
Ooooooh baby, here I am, signed, sealed, delivered,
*   I'm yours.*

"This sounds familiar," I said. "What is it?"

JP stopped his knife in midslice as he spun to look at me. "Sounds *familiar*? What the hell planet have you been living on?! You really don't know who this is?" I hesitated, then shook my head. JP made the sign of the cross and turned to Lisa.

"It's Stevie Wonder," she said.

"Thank you! Yai yai yai." JP shook his knife at me. "You be grateful. If she hadn't known, you'd both be eating hot dogs in the parking lot. You've got a lot to learn, that's for sure."

He switched on the gas stovetop, tossed some oil into a pan and in a matter of what seemed like seconds, he'd chopped up some garlic and thrown it onto the heat. I was hypnotized by the unfamiliar aromas. Working smoothly, almost in time to the music, and occasionally reaching over to take a healthy swig from his wineglass, JP added vegetables to the pan, tossed in white wine, cream and some cooked pasta. Before we knew it, he was filling our plates, topping them with ground pepper and sliding them across the stainless steel counter toward us.

I took a bite, and for a moment all I was aware of was the food. It was like nothing I'd ever tasted—rich and smooth and absolutely delicious. For a few minutes, there was complete silence as we devoured the pasta.

Lisa let out a deep and satisfied sigh and said, "Aren't you going to eat anything, JP?" He waved her off.

"You'll soon realize that JP survives on cigarettes and red wine," said Denise. "Now why don't you kids get out of here? Tomorrow's a big day. You should go home and try to get some sleep." I started to gather up the dishes and take them over to the sink to wash, but she stopped me. "Don't worry about it, Dan. JP and I will finish cleaning up. Lisa, can you give Danny a ride home?"

"Sure."

I'd been hoping something like this would happen. Until now, Denise had driven me home every night after work. Maybe some time alone with Lisa would help me figure out what she really thought of me.

In the parking lot, as Lisa rummaged around in her bag for her keys, I could hear Denise and JP laughing on the deck. The faint aroma of sweet-smelling smoke wafted toward us on the summer breeze.

"Is that pot?" I asked, hoping I didn't sound like a supernerd.

"Yeah, big surprise, eh? I bet those crazy old hippies couldn't wait to get us out of there so they could blaze up. Aha!" She pulled the keys triumphantly out of her bag.

I waited outside the car for a minute while she quickly threw tapes, books, makeup and clothes into the backseat.

"Sorry! I've been pretty much living out of this thing. Hop in."

"Did you drive this car all the way up from New York?" I asked as I wedged myself in amidst the clutter.

"You mean Old Bessie here? No way. I never would have made it all the way here in this piece of shit. It's my aunt's. This thing has been rusting out in her backyard for years. She's letting me use it for the summer."

She turned the key, and the engine made a horrible grinding sound before finally turning over.

"Good girl!" She patted the dashboard appreciatively.

I gave her directions to my house, and she peeled out of the parking lot. I tried not to pay attention to the erratic clanging and rattling noises that seemed to come from all corners of the car.

"Man," I said as we headed out of town, "that pasta was delicious!"

She shrugged. "Yeah, it was okay. JP is a decent chef. Definitely not the best I've worked with though."

Maybe she was right, but the meal JP had prepared was easily the best thing I'd ever eaten. I couldn't wait to find out what else he could do in the kitchen.

"So," she said, "tell me about your love life. Got your eyes on anyone special?"

My heart fluttered. Was she asking just to be polite, or did she have deeper motives?

"Wha—me? No. I mean, I dated this girl, Michelle, for a while, but it didn't really work out."

She nodded and kept driving.

"How about you?" I asked.

"Nope." I waited for her to elaborate, but she didn't say anything else.

She pulled into the driveway.

"Here ya go, sailor," she said. "Big day tomorrow."

I turned to her and smiled, and she smiled back. For a brief moment, I imagined reaching over and putting my hand on her face, leaning in and kissing her. Maybe all I had to do was make one little move, and everything else would fall into place. Instead, I opened the door and jumped out of the car, and she pulled away with a short honk of her horn, her hand waving cheerfully out the window.

I stood and watched as Old Bessie clattered away. *What's wrong with me?* I thought as her headlights disappeared into the night.

EIGHT

The next morning, after I got out of the shower and came back to my room, Alma was sitting on my bed.

"What's up?" I asked her.

"Do you think that I could get a job at the restaurant? As a waitress?" she asked me.

"Maybe in a few years, Al," I said, drying off my hair. "You're kind of young. Trust me, having a job isn't all it's cracked up to be."

"Yeah, but I've been thinking about running away to Hollywood in a couple of years to become an actress," she said. "It'd be good to have some skills, like waiting tables. I'll probably need to make ends meet for a few weeks, until I'm discovered. God knows I don't want to end up like Peg Entwhistle."

"Who's Peg Entwhistle?"

"Oh, just a tragic ingenue from the thirties," she said. "She couldn't catch a break, so she climbed up to the Hollywood sign and—ack!" She crossed her eyes and stuck out her tongue, holding an imaginary noose above her neck.

"Yoinks," I said.

"Yoinks indeed, but what did she expect? Who the hell is going to hire someone called Peg Entwhistle? She might as well have called herself Velma Turnipgarden. I'm going to stick with my original stage name."

"Oh yes," I said, "Betsy Worthington. Well, in a couple of years, I'll put in a good word with Denise. In the meantime, enjoy the free ride while you can, Betsy."

"Can you guys come down here?" Mom called from downstairs.

"I have some news," she said when we were sitting down. "Your dad's going to be home at the end of the month."

"What?" said Alma. "That's awesome!"

"I don't understand," I said. "I thought his contract lasted till Christmas."

"Well, that's the thing," she said. "His company is laying off a bunch of people, so it's not really good news."

Great, I thought, another opportunity for him to lecture me about the importance of education. Same old story, blah, blah, blah.

"He gets to come home for the rest of the summer though!" said Alma. "*That's* good news!"

"Yes, that will be nice, for sure," my mom said, reaching over to run her fingers through Alma's hair.

"Mom!" Alma said. "'Take your stinkin' paws off me, you damn dirty ape!'"

"He's very impressed that you're working so hard at the restaurant, Dan," Mom said, turning to me.

"Oh yeah? Cool." It actually *was* cool. For once in my life, I could prove I was thinking about my future. So far, I'd only had one payday, but I'd put most of it in the bank, and I planned to keep saving. By the time Dad came home, I'd have a few hundred bucks. I was sure he'd have lots of ideas about how I should spend it.

WHEN I ARRIVED at the restaurant for my shift later that day, Denise was giving a tour of the place to a couple of people. One of them was a university student named Ken who I recognized as a DCHS grad from a couple of years earlier. He was taller than me and well built, with an earring and bleached tips. Denise introduced him to everyone, and he barely glanced at me and JP other than to give us a quick nod. I noticed that he was a lot friendlier to Lisa, cracking cheesy jokes and reaching out to touch her on the arm a couple of times.

The other server turned out to be Maisie Thomas.

"Hey, Maisie! I didn't know you were going to be working here," I said.

"Yeah, it's awesome, hey? I'm super excited!" She giggled. "It's going to be a super fun summer!"

Behind Maisie's back, Lisa caught my eye and raised her eyebrows, smirking. I really liked Maisie and figured she'd be great with customers, but I had a feeling that she wasn't really Lisa's kind of person.

My suspicions were confirmed a bit later when Lisa came into the kitchen to help me polish some silverware. "So are you like, *super best friends* with Anne of Green Gables back there?" she asked.

"You mean Maisie?" I shrugged. "I don't really hang out with her or anything. She's really nice though."

"Nice," said Lisa. "Nice is what people say when they can't come up with a better word to describe someone. Maybe you mean boring. Or dumb."

"I didn't say that!" I said, surprised at her suddenly nasty tone. Then she snapped back to her normal self, laughing and flicking a dishcloth at me.

"Don't get your knickers in a knot, I'm sure she's a really sweet person. You and I just have a lot more in common."

Denise yelled to us through the window to come out to the parking lot, and I followed Lisa outside, wondering what she'd meant. Was she jealous of Maisie? I decided to take it as a promising sign.

Denise and JP had hung the new sign over the door, a colorful painting of a sunset with *The Sandbar* painted above it. JP passed out plastic cups, and Denise walked around filling them with sparkling wine.

Denise raised her glass and said, "To a lucky first season. Let's hope it all works out!" We clinked our glasses and cheered, and then JP clapped his hands sharply, twice.

"All right. We gotta get goin' or there won't be any food for the people."

We snapped into action, and soon I was in the kitchen tying on an apron, facing a deep sink full of soapy water and a counter that was ready to be stacked with greasy dishes.

By the time the restaurant had been open for a couple of hours, I was already wondering what I'd gotten myself into. To begin with, the place was packed, and although Lisa, Maisie and Ken were all waiting tables, it seemed as if they couldn't get to people fast enough. Denise was doing triple duty, trying to pick up the slack in the dining room, running in to help in the kitchen whenever she had a second, and ringing customers through at the front counter.

The orders came piling into the kitchen in an endless stream, and soon enough the dishes followed. For every carefully arranged plate that was taken away, it seemed as if three came back piled high with garbage. More than once, I had to force myself not to gag as I scraped chicken bones, congealed piles of cold pasta, even spit-out pieces of gum into a revolting pile in the garbage can next to the sink. I did my best to keep up, but it was a tough battle, and I didn't really know what I was doing. Denise had promised to give me a lesson, but we'd been so busy, she hadn't gotten around to it. Thankfully, JP was totally cool under pressure, and he helped me stay on track by calling firm, clear orders in my direction.

"I'm gonna need two fry pans and a big stainless bowl in a couple of minutes!"

Before I knew it, I was up to my eyeballs in dirty dishes. I had just started to get a routine going, stacking dirty plates and dinnerware to the left of the sink and pots and pans and cooking tools to the right, when Denise marched up behind me, picked up a huge pile of dishes and dumped them all into the sink. Then she reached around me, grabbed a bunch of pots and tossed them in as well.

"You're wasting time, Danny. This isn't rocket science. You take the pots and pans, you drop them in the water as fast as they come, you scrub, you hustle them back to JP's station. You take plates and glasses, you give them a quick rinse, you throw them in the dishwasher, you repeat. *Capiche*?"

I nodded, and she stalked away. I dropped my head, focusing on the water as I furiously scrubbed at the dishes, taking out my frustrations on the grease. It wasn't like I'd done this kind of thing before, and she sure hadn't given me much of an intro. I didn't have time to think about it, though, and so I tried to just keep getting stuff to JP as he needed it.

Unfortunately, it was easier said than done. The dishes kept coming at me twice as fast as I could wash them. Although he stayed calm, I could see that JP was trying to keep things moving and that every time he had to stop to wait for dishes, it ruined his flow.

The only enjoyable thing about the kitchen in full work mode was the smell. One mouth-watering aroma after another wafted by me from JP's workspace near the stove. Whenever possible, I tried to turn around and see what he was doing, but I was so busy that I only managed to grab a few glimpses: chicken on rice, smothered with a yellow sauce—curry, maybe?—and topped with chopped nuts and a sprig of herbs; steaks with a pan sauce and a pile of potatoes under a teepee of green beans; golden seared scallops covered with finely diced mangos. I wished I could just stand next to JP and watch what he was doing, instead of being stuck in the disgusting dish pit.

Lisa came into the kitchen and stuck her head over my shoulder.

"Having fun?" she asked.

"What does it look like?" I said. "This sucks."

She laughed. "You'll be fine, don't worry. Nobody out there is complaining. I don't think anyone in this town has ever eaten real food before. They don't mind waiting for clean dishes."

Ken wasn't as accommodating. Every time he had to wait for an order because the dishes weren't ready, he stood behind me with his arms crossed, sighing deeply. The only thing it accomplished was to make me tense. At one point, while waiting impatiently for four orders of mussels, he actually reached behind me and grabbed plates from my drying rack.

"Get it together, guy," he growled. "You'd think you never washed a dish before in your life." I had a feeling he and I weren't going to be best friends.

The next few hours were about as much fun as a nail in the forehead, but eventually things quieted down a bit, and the pile of dirty dishes diminished. JP stepped outside to grab a smoke while there were no orders on the line, and when he stepped back into the kitchen, the dish pit was clean for the first time all evening.

"Look at you, kid. Maybe you've got some skills after all."

"I'm not so sure about that," I said. As much as I appreciated him trying to make me feel better, I felt like a total loser. I should have been faster...better...more efficient. If I couldn't even do this right, it was no wonder I couldn't figure out what to do with my life.

Finally the last customers left, the door was locked, and the servers finished clearing the dining room. While I washed the last few pots and pans, Lisa and Maisie hung out in the kitchen, laughing at JP's jokes. Ken had taken off immediately after work.

Denise came in from tallying up the night's receipts and sidled up next to me at the sink.

"This is why I wanted JP to come work for me," she told me, tilting her head toward them. "Not only is JP a damn good chef, he can make the most insane kitchen a fun place to work." She slapped me on the back. "Don't worry, Dan. You'll get better as time goes on. It's all about the learning curve, buddy."

She yelled across the kitchen. "All right, guys, that was a good first night, and we only had a few fires to put out. Now everyone go home and get some sleep. We're going to do it all again tomorrow."

NINE

I hated washing dishes with a passion. At night in bed, I'd close my eyes only to see food slops and dirty dishes flying past my head into an endless sink of grimy water, full of soggy bread crusts and slimy lettuce leaves. It was disgusting, unrewarding work, and to top it all off, my legs and back were killing me.

The only thing that got me through the days was the promise of hanging out with Lisa after work. Once the restaurant was cleaned and locked up every night, we'd get in Old Bessie and drive around for hours, listening to Lisa's mix tapes and talking about anything and everything, although it was usually Lisa doing the talking.

The more she described living in New York, the more I wanted to get there as soon as possible.

Lisa seemed to feel the opposite way. She loved how quiet and remote Deep Cove was, and she always wanted to explore old dirt roads or hidden beaches that I'd taken for granted my whole life. A couple of times she asked if I wanted to meet up with any of my friends, but I made lame excuses about how busy they were. The truth was that both Jay and Kierce had left messages at my house, but I hadn't called them back. I wanted to keep Lisa to myself, at least until I figured out what was going on between us.

We'd been working together for almost two weeks, but I still couldn't tell how she felt about me. I wasn't in a huge rush to find out. I liked things the way they were. I wished this was all there was to being her boyfriend: totally connecting, but no stupid sex stuff getting in the way. Sometimes I thought she might be into me, other times, I wasn't so sure. She talked about old boyfriends, guys she'd slept with, men she had major crushes on. One night she even told me that she thought Ken was hot.

"Oh god," I said. "Do you really? He's such a dick."

"Yeah, but girls like jerks. They're sexy. Too bad he has a girlfriend. Don't worry though, Danny, I still think you're cuter," she said, reaching over to ruffle my hair.

What did she mean, *cuter*? It was so confusing, trying to figure out what was going on in her head.

Worst of all, I knew what she meant about Ken. He was a total asshole, but he *was* pretty hot. His muscles filled out his T-shirt, he had a great tan and his hair was perfectly tousled. I wondered what he'd look like with his shirt off. In his underwear. Naked. I hated myself for thinking about him that way. I was supposed to be thinking about Lisa instead, but that just wasn't happening.

I knew I had to turn things around. I refused to admit defeat—the alternative was too awful to think about.

ON MY FIRST DAY off since starting my job, I got on my bike and rode to the Spot. I didn't know if I'd find what I was looking for, but sure enough it was there, rolled into a tube and wedged into a crack at the upper edge of the back wall.

Luscious. A sleazy porno Jay had stolen from his uncle and brought to the Spot a few years back. Most of the magazine was familiar to me. I'd sat around with the guys pretending to find it exciting, back when we all still had the same number of notches in our belts—which was none. Really though, I'd hated it. Porn was so stupid. Why the hell would a naked girl on a bicycle need a fur hat?

The magazine had been forgotten for at least a couple of years. It was damp and mildewed, and when I unrolled it, wood bugs scurried out from the pages. I smacked it against the cement to knock them off, and flipped through it, trying to understand what it was that got other guys hot and horny.

One ridiculous-looking girl after another smiled up at me with big eyes and teased hair—coy and inviting, everything out in the open for me to look at. I forced myself to examine the pictures carefully, but all I could feel was embarrassment for them. They had too much makeup on, their hair was too big, they weren't wearing any clothes. Didn't these girls have families? Jesus.

I tried to picture Lisa lying on a bearskin rug with her mouth parted slightly, arching her back with her legs spread, running her hands through her hair, waiting for... Waiting for what? I knew what she was waiting for, but when I tried to put myself into the scene, I wasn't giving it to her. Instead, I imagined running at her with a blanket, averting my eyes, telling her to cover up. I wasn't off to a good start.

I flipped through a few more pages and came to a photo spread that I remembered clearly. *Sapphire and Chaz: On the High Seas.* Sapphire was a sullen brunette with gigantic boobs spilling out of a wench costume.

Totally tacky. Chaz, on the other hand, was a bona fide hunk. Tall and muscular, with a chiseled jaw and a mane of white-blond hair tied back with a tattered ribbon. His pirate costume unlaced to his waist, his gigantic—

"Hey, Danny!"

I heard footsteps above me, and suddenly someone was sliding down the hill toward the Spot. I quickly rolled the magazine up and shoved it back into its hiding place, and a moment later Jay hoisted himself up and joined me on the ledge.

"What's up, man?" he said, reaching over to give me a high five. He looked so happy to see me that I immediately felt guilty about having avoided him for so long.

"How's it going?" I asked, trying to sound casual, although my heart was racing from almost being discovered.

"I saw your bike up there. What are you doing here?"

"Got the day off, thought I'd go for a spin. I was gonna come see if you were home in a few minutes."

He rolled his eyes. "Trust me, that's the last place you want to be right now. I got into it with my mom. Women are crazy."

"Yeah," I said. He didn't know the half of it. "What happened?"

"Oh you know, same old bullshit." He put on a fake shrill voice, "*You need to get your act together or you'll end up digging ditches like your uncle!*" He laughed. "What's the big deal, right? Digging ditches isn't the end of the world. Build some muscle, work outside all day, smoke all you want." He pulled out a cigarette and lit up.

"Yeah, I know where you're coming from," I said. "My old man's coming home in a couple of weeks. He'll be giving me a hard time too."

"Yeah, I'm sure that'll kind of suck, but it's not really the same thing. At least you have good marks. You can do something with your life." His face fell briefly. Weird. I'd never really thought Jay worried about school or his future. A second later, he was smiling again.

"So how's work going anyway, man?" he asked.

"It's good. Well, not the actual work—dishwashing sucks, by the way—but the people are cool." I hesitated for a minute, wondering if I should say anything about Lisa. "There's kind of a…girl, that I work with, and she's pretty cool."

"No way!" he said. "I was wondering why we hadn't seen you lately. That's awesome, man!"

"Yeah, I guess so."

"What do you mean, you guess so? What's the problem?"

"Well, I don't know if she likes me," I said.

"Well, give it a shot. What's the worst that can happen? She's not interested? Big deal, right?"

"Yeah, I don't know. Can I ask you a question?"

"Shoot."

"When you first—you know—with Della, were you nervous?" Della Klein had been Jay's first. A year ago, they'd gone all the way behind the school ball field. Jay's smile had been even bigger than usual for about a week afterward.

"Yeah, sure, but it's not like it's all that complicated. You just kind of *do it*, right?"

"Sure, yeah."

"It's easier than English class, that's for sure." He laughed. "I wish I could have been graded on sex with Della. I don't think I would have gotten an A plus or anything, but I definitely would have passed." He grinned and stubbed out his smoke on the concrete.

"Here's what I think, Dan," he went on. "Rule Number One: Don't ever listen to Kierce. I love the guy, but he's a total douche bag, especially about girls, and he doesn't know nearly as much as he thinks he does. Just relax and let things happen."

He rummaged around in his backpack and held up two condoms in foil wrappers.

"You got some of these?"

"Uh, no."

He tossed them at me. "Keep 'em. Hope springs eternal, or whatever, right?"

"Shakespeare?"

"Who the fuck knows? Listen, don't put any pressure on yourself, dude. Just wait till it's the right time. I kind of regret doing it so early."

"Really?"

"Nah, not really." He laughed. "But you're way more sensitive about stuff like that."

"Do me a favor, will you?" I asked him. "Don't tell Kierce about any of this."

"Sure, but why not?"

"I just don't want him to know until I can figure out if it's gonna happen or not."

"Suit yourself. But, Danny?"

"Yeah?"

"Try not to take everything so seriously, will ya?"

TEN

Despite Jay's advice, I couldn't stop thinking about Kierce's rules. *Rule 264: All you need is a sick mind and a healthy body. Rule 15: Girls always want guys to make the first move. Rule 78: Time waits for no man.* I knew that one was true. If I wanted something to happen, I had to just do it.

The night after I talked to Jay, I directed Lisa to a dark dirt road outside of town and got her to park at the end of an old lane. We fought our way through tangles of wild rose bushes to a little grassy meadow at the top of a hill. There was a full view of the ocean and, off in the distance, the lights of Deep Cove seemed to blend seamlessly into the starlit sky above. It was the most romantic place I could think of, and I knew we wouldn't be bothered there. In my back pocket was one of the condoms Jay had given me.

"Wow," said Lisa when we got to the top, "this place is beautiful!"

"Yeah. My parents used to take me here to pick berries when I was a kid."

"No way. You really had a Tom Sawyer childhood, didn't you?" She walked over to the edge of the tall grass and sat down. I followed, and we sat side by side, gazing out at the night in front of us. She lit a cigarette, and for a long time neither of us said anything.

"I never told you about my mom, did I?" Lisa was almost whispering when she broke the silence.

"No. Well, you said she had some issues, or something like that."

She laughed. Not a happy laugh. "Yeah, well I guess you could say that. Basically, she's fucking crazy."

I didn't know how to respond to that, so I didn't say anything.

"When I was a kid, she was always normal, or at least I thought she was. She loved to take my brother and me to museums or to the zoo in Central Park, that kind of thing. When she was in a good mood, she laughed all the time, and she and my dad were always kissing and joking around and stuff. Every year we'd go on a big family vacation. France, Japan, all kinds of places. Anyway, as long as she was happy, we were all happy..."

She stubbed out her cigarette and was quiet for a bit before continuing.

"But once in a while, my mom would just kind of—disappear. She wouldn't leave our apartment. She'd just get really distant, and sometimes she'd go into her room and close the door, and we wouldn't see her for a while. My dad never said much about it. He'd be like, 'Your mom has a headache.' Stuff like that. Usually it would only last a few days, then we'd wake up and she'd be in the kitchen, smiling and making breakfast like nothing had happened. Will—that's my brother—he and I just thought...I guess we thought it was normal.

"So then, one day when I was about eight and Will was almost twelve, my dad went away on a business trip to Chicago. For a day or so she seemed fine, but then she locked herself in her room and wouldn't come out when we were there. Thank god my brother was there. We had no idea how to get in touch with my dad, but Will found her purse and took money out to order us pizza."

"She didn't come out of her room? Did you try to talk to her?" The whole thing sounded almost unbelievable to me. My parents could be super annoying, but I knew they would never deliberately neglect us.

"Oh, yeah. We'd call through the door. We must have tried the doorknob a hundred times. Nothing. We knew she wasn't dead, or whatever. We'd hear her moving around, and the water would run in her bathroom every so often. But she wouldn't say anything. It was really scary."

"How long was she in there?"

"A week."

"Oh my god! Wow. So what happened?"

"Well, we went to school every day because Will was worried that if we didn't show up, our parents would get in trouble or something. Finally our dad came home. He could tell as soon as he walked into the apartment that something wasn't right, and he went straight to the bedroom and banged on the door. She let him in, and he was in there for a long time. The next day, we came home from school and she was gone. Off to a mental hospital. For two months."

"Wow," I said again.

"So anyway, eventually she came home, and she seemed a lot better, and there were lots of apologies. She explained to us that she had been sick, but now she had medicine that was making her better, and that was it. She was fine for a long time, and then last year she started to act weird again. Will had already moved away to university, and I was out with my friends all the time, and nobody really noticed. I guess she stopped taking her meds. Who knows why."

"What about your dad?"

"Dad was away on business a lot, and then when she started to act weird again, he said he'd had enough and he just kind of picked up and left for good. Pretty weak, I guess, but hard to blame him. Anyway, that's when she really went off the deep end."

She looked at me, almost apologetically. "Am I boring you with this?"

"No! Not at all, seriously!"

"A couple of months ago, she OD'd on sleeping pills. We'd had a big fight, and I'd gone to stay at Naomi's place, but Will happened to come home for the weekend and found her, and got her to the hospital in time."

She gave me a crooked smile, but I could see that her eyes were wet. She wiped the back of her hand across her face and took a deep breath.

"Long story short, that's why I'm here for the summer. My Aunt Cheryl flew in and helped Will arrange everything, and my mom went off to the loony bin again. Then I came here for the summer. I didn't want to," she said. "Especially so soon after she got out of the hospital.

I felt guilty. I thought I should stay with her. But Will and Cheryl insisted. They said I deserved to get away for a while and have some time to myself, and that it wasn't up to me to look after her."

"Yeah. For sure." I was finding it hard to think of anything appropriate to say. *Sorry your mom's nuts* didn't seem like the right response.

"I know it makes me sound like such a bitch," she said, "but the whole thing just pisses me off. It's like, did she even think about me at all?"

I nodded. I knew it must have been really hard on her, but it didn't sound to me as if her mom had done any of it deliberately. She obviously had some real mental issues, and Lisa seemed to be going easy on her dad. But what did I know? My parents were pretty normal, all things considered. My own problems paled in comparison to this stuff. It was like something out of a movie. Central Park? Mental hospitals?

She threw her arms out in front of her with mock enthusiasm. "So here I am! Stuck in the middle of nowhere! I'm sorry for unloading my shit on you. It's just tough to talk to Cheryl about it. She's been so awesome already, I don't want her to feel that she has to be my shrink or something."

She jumped up, then reached down to grab my hands and pull me up.

"Thanks so much for listening to me, Danny. It means a lot."

She pulled me into a hug and held on for a long time, with her head on my shoulder. I turned and buried my face in her hair, and the world stopped moving for a few moments. Everything became quiet and still. The stars were thick in the sky, the air was warm and sweet, her hair smelled incredible. I knew that if I was going to kiss her, this was the perfect opportunity. I pulled my head back slowly to look at her, and she looked up at me, smiling.

I thought about what Jay had said—*just do it*. But it was no use. Her voice was soft, her breath smelled like cherry lip gloss, and her breasts were pressed up against my chest. This wasn't what I wanted.

"Do you know what I like about you?" she asked, pulling away and looking at me with a crooked smile.

"What?" I asked, my head spinning.

"You're not always trying to get into my pants like every other pervert dude I've ever met." She laughed. "*That* is an excellent trait in a guy."

What would she think if I told her I was another kind of pervert altogether?

She smiled brightly and reached up to mess with my bangs. "We should probably hit the road; it's getting late," she said. Then she turned and ran back down the hill in big flying leaps, laughing the whole way.

I followed her at a distance, battling two emotions: relief that nothing had happened, and disgust with myself for feeling relieved.

ELEVEN

I was a failure. A fraud. A homo. A queer. A fag. Gay.

I knew that in other parts of the world, being gay wasn't such a big deal. There were gay bars, gay businesses, even whole gay neighborhoods. There were gay doctors and gay lawyers and gay actors and gay musicians. In big cities like New York and Toronto and San Francisco, there were gay pride parades, full of gay people covered with gay glitter and gay feathers dancing to gay music. Those people looked happy, like they could afford to have fun and be themselves.

But none of that mattered, because none of those people lived in Deep Cove.

Was I supposed to throw myself a one-man pride parade? I pictured myself zooming down Main Street on a pink bicycle wearing a feather boa, dodging rotten tomatoes and the jeers of everyone I'd ever known. I imagined Kierce and Ferris and their hockey buddies beating the shit out of me. I saw Jay looking at me with disgust and never speaking to me again. I wondered how my family would react if they ever found out. Would my parents disown me? Would Alma be so embarrassed that she'd pretend she didn't even have a brother?

I was an island of gayness in an ocean of straightness.

The way I saw it, I had two options. I could try to be somebody other than myself for the rest of my life, or I could pick up and move far away. It was obvious that Plan A had failed miserably. If Lisa couldn't turn me on, there wasn't a girl on earth who could change me. It wasn't going to happen. Period. Full stop.

That left me with Plan B. I had to get out of Deep Cove, move as far away as I could, because there was no way I could tell anyone here who I really was. To hell with figuring out a career plan for after high school. What I needed was an escape route.

To make matters worse, things at the restaurant were getting shittier by the day. I couldn't seem to get any faster at washing dishes. Every time I felt like I was getting somewhere, a huge load of dishes would come in from the dining room, or the dishwasher would malfunction, leaving me soaked and the dishes still dirty.

When I fell behind, JP always kept his cool, but I knew I was holding him up. Luckily, the customers didn't seem to mind waiting for their food. We were packed every night, and the Sandbar was getting rave reviews. It was great that the restaurant was doing well, but it didn't make me feel any better about being the weak link.

A couple of evenings after my night on the hill with Lisa, I was crossing the kitchen with a stack of plates, fresh out of the dishwasher. JP turned around quickly with a hot pan of food, and when I moved to get out of his way, I tripped, and the plates flew out of my hands. I watched in horror as they landed on the service counter and smashed into a million pieces. Shards of broken pottery sprinkled a row of freshly plated entrees that JP had just put up for one of Ken's tables. I froze as Denise came rushing into the kitchen, followed closely by Ken.

"What was that?" she asked. Then she saw the mess I'd made. She covered her face with her hands. "Danny, Danny, Danny. What the…No, I can't deal with this right now." She turned around and walked out of the kitchen. I looked at JP, who had quickly turned back to the stove to remake the orders.

"Okay, guy," he said. "Scrape those plates into the garbage, and then sweep it up. Pronto."

"Way to go, guy," Ken sneered. "Now I get to explain to the customers why their food isn't ready yet." He gave the swinging door a heavy smack on his way back out to the dining room. I lifted my middle finger at his back, and was momentarily pleased to hear JP chuckle.

I felt like shit, but there was no time to stop and feel sorry for myself. I did as he told me and got the mess cleaned up, then dove back into the dish pit and tried my best to get things under control. JP managed to pull everything together in short order, and soon enough, things were back on track.

"Don't worry, guy," he said. "Everyone has accidents. That's the business for you."

Somehow that didn't make me feel any better. The rest of the shift seemed to drag on forever, and Denise didn't look at me for the rest of the evening.

The next day, when I got to work, I found her giving a tour of the kitchen to Parker, a sullen younger kid I recognized from school. She was explaining how to use the dishwasher.

"Hey, Dan," she said. "Why don't you go wait in the dining room for me." I went out and sat at one of the tables, my chin in my hands. I figured I was lucky to have lasted this long. I couldn't blame Denise if she fired me; I was a total disaster as a dishwasher. After a few minutes, she came out and sat across the table from me.

"So, this probably won't surprise you," she said, "but the whole dishwashing thing just isn't working out. I hate to say it, buddy, but you are definitely not cut out for the dish pit."

"It's okay," I said, trying not to sound as miserable as I felt. I moved to stand up from the table. "Thanks a lot for giving me a chance. It was really cool working for you."

"Hang on," she said, "where are you going? I didn't say you were fired, I said you were a terrible dishwasher."

I didn't understand. "Do you want me to wait tables?"

"Hell, no. If you were even half as bad at that as you were at washing dishes, this place wouldn't last a week. No, I was thinking that I'd put you to work with JP."

"Really?"

"He's really been slammed, and I can tell that he's only barely keeping his shit together. I'm pretty sure if I don't get him some help soon, he's going to quit, and then we're all screwed."

"Do you think JP will be okay working with me?"

"Actually, it was his idea. He thinks part of the reason that you are such a shitty dishwasher is that you spend half your time watching him cook, so we might as well put you where you might actually learn something."

I felt as if I'd won the lottery. Big-time.

The next morning, I came to work an hour early so JP could give me a rundown of some basics.

"Okay," he said, "first things first. You don't touch my knives. You touch my knives, I cut your thumbs off, I go to jail, Denise has to close the restaurant, you have no thumbs, and nobody wins."

JP's knives were his babies. He'd transported them from Montreal in a metal briefcase that looked like it held a nuclear detonator, and he kept them next to the stove in a wooden block.

He reached up to a shelf and pulled down a stained, tied-up bundle of cloth. "Go ahead," he said, dropping it in front of me, "unroll it."

It was a set of five knives, much older and more beat up than the ones he used. The handles were mismatched, and there were spots of rust on some of them.

"This is my backup set. I used these way back when I was a young kitchen slave, like you. You can use them for the summer. They don't look like much, but they're good knives. These are real steel; none of that stainless bullshit. That's why they're kind of rusty. You have to keep them clean and dry, and you rub oil onto them every night before you leave the kitchen."

"Cool," I said. They were pretty shitty-looking knives, but I wasn't about to complain. Anything to keep me out of the dish pit.

JP grabbed a ten-pound bag of potatoes from the corner and dropped it on the counter in front of me.

"First lesson." He picked up the smallest knife in the bundle. "This is your paring knife. Small, but very important. This little guy will do delicate work, like making garnishes, and it can do stuff that bigger knives can't, like getting the seeds out of a pepper. But first things first." He sliced open the bag of potatoes, grabbed one and peeled it perfectly in about ten seconds. He did another one, slower, showing me how to hold the knife and move the potato, and then he got me to try. I was slow and choppy, and cut several chunks out of the potato in the process.

"Wouldn't it be a lot easier to use a peeler?" I asked.

"Oh yes, much easier. But what would you learn?" He patted me on the back. "You do this whole bag, and then we'll see what's next."

I looked at the gigantic bag of potatoes, took a deep breath and started peeling.

JP was right; by the time I'd peeled twenty pounds of potatoes, I felt as if I'd actually learned something. Over the next couple of days, I peeled what felt like hundreds of carrots and thousands of potatoes. It was boring and repetitive, but I kind of enjoyed the rhythm of it, and by the end of a few days of nonstop peeling, I felt as if I really knew how to use that paring knife.

Over the next week, I slowly graduated to doing more complicated prep work. I wasn't actually learning to cook yet, but I knew the difference between a slice, a dice and a julienne. Depending on what JP needed for a particular dish, I did plenty of all three.

JP showed me how to pull the hairy little beards out of mussels, and how to devein a shrimp. I used my hands to break apart endless heads of romaine lettuce, wash out all the dirt, and rip them into little pieces for Caesar salad. I learned to crush cloves of garlic with the palm of my hand so that they would slide right out of their skin, and to mince them into tiny piles of fragrant mush that went into almost everything JP cooked.

The kitchen had become fun again. Now that I was helping him, JP was able to relax a bit. When he was relaxed, he listened to music. Lots of music. When we had a rush, and things in the kitchen were really intense, he'd listen to the Clash or the Stones. When things were calmer and running smoothly, he listened to hippie music, like Van Morrison or Joni Mitchell. But his standby was definitely Stevie Wonder, who quickly became my favorite too. When Stevie's happy seventies beats rolled out of *le boom box*, I found it impossible not to tap my feet.

Parker tuned out JP's music with giant headphones, plugged into a Walkman that was turned up so high that we could hear the muffled sounds of Green Day or NOFX buzzing around his head. He only communicated when he absolutely had to, and then only with grunts and shrugs. That didn't bother anyone though, because he turned out to be a much better dishwasher than I'd ever be. He stood scowling at the sink, attacking the dish pit with gusto and angrily nodding his head along to his music.

Out in the dining room, things were also going well. Lisa told me that they were making pretty good tips, and Maisie was her usual cheerful self. Denise didn't say much; she had a lot on her plate. But she always had a slight smile on her face, so I assumed that she was happy with the way things were going.

Ken continued to rub me the wrong way. He wasn't friendly to me at all, although he flirted constantly with Lisa and Maisie. He was totally full of himself and would ramble on and on about pretentious crap like the bouquet of a charming Zinfandel. Worst of all, he was constantly making suggestions to JP in the kitchen.

"You know," he said, "if you chop up some parsley to sprinkle over the bruschetta when it comes out of the oven, it will really improve the presentation."

JP smiled and nodded. "That's an idea. I'll think about that." He didn't follow Ken's advice on that or anything else. The customers didn't seem to mind that the bruschetta didn't have parsley on it; they ordered tons of it, and the plates always came back empty.

Sometimes, when I was hard at work in the kitchen and the music was playing, I could almost forget that I was counting down the days till I could leave Deep Cove forever and start a new life somewhere else.

TWELVE

I was in the middle of chopping a pile of onions one night almost three weeks after the Sandbar opened, when Denise came over to my workstation. "You've got a couple of admirers out in the dining room," she told me. "Go ahead, take a break."

Kierce and Jay were sitting by a window at a table for two. I grabbed a seat from an empty table and pulled it over to sit with them.

"Nice apron, Chef Boyardee," said Kierce, reaching over to grab the strap.

"What are you guys doing here?"

"Don't be tho thilly," he said, flopping his wrist around. "Me and Jay-Jay wanted to have a thekthy date night, jutht the two of uth." He reached over the table and tried to grab Jay's hand.

"Cut it out, you freak!" said Jay, swatting him away. "We wanted to see what this place was all about." He looked down at his plate of pasta. "It's no BS, but it's pretty good."

"Besides," said Kierce, "we wondered if we were ever going to see you again."

"Yeah, I know," I said. "It's been really busy."

"No problemo, man," said Kierce. "Gotta make a dollar, right?" He lowered his voice. "Who's our waitress? She's like a linebacker or something."

"That's Denise, my boss. She's cool."

"Yeah, cool like a cold shower. She's gotta be a dyke."

I felt sickness and rage start to boil in my stomach. Couldn't he just forget about that stuff for ten seconds?

"Cut it out, Kierce," I said. "You're being a dick."

"Thorry." He looked past me, and his eyes widened. "Who the hell is *that*? I wish *she* was our waitress."

I turned around, already knowing who he was looking at.

"That's Lisa."

"Are you banging her yet?" asked Kierce.

"No," I said, "we're just friends. She drives me home after work sometimes, that's all."

Jay shot me a quick look that I assumed meant, *What are you doing, man*? I shrugged at him.

Kierce reached over and gave me a shot in the arm. "Dibs on that fine ass, man. Rule Thirty-nine: You snooze, you lose." He put his hand up and waved at her. "Excuse me, miss!" he said.

"Kierce, what the hell are you doing?" I asked him.

"Relax," he said. "Watch and learn from the master, boys."

"Would that be Master Bates?" asked Jay.

Lisa walked over to the table. "Hey, can I help you guys?"

Kierce stood up and stuck out his hand. "Since Danny won't introduce us, I figured I'd have to do it myself. I'm Kierce, and this is Jay. We're Danny's crew. His boys. His posse."

"Ooh, Dan," she said, shaking Kierce's hand, "I didn't know you had a posse!" She smiled at them. "I'm Lisa."

"You're obviously very busy, Lisa," Kierce went on, "but we wanted to ask if you would be willing to hang out with us sometime."

I glared at him across the table.

"That sounds great," she said. "How about tomorrow after D and I finish our shift?"

"Rule Fourteen, boys," said Kierce, after she'd moved on to another table. "When opportunity knocks, open the door and invite her in."

AFTER WORK THE NEXT NIGHT, we picked the guys up in Lisa's car. They were standing outside Jay's house when we showed up, and she surprised all of us by veering Old Bessie directly toward them and leaning on the horn. She slammed on the brakes and came to an abrupt stop a good ten feet away, but not before they'd both leaped out of the way, looks of shock plastered across their faces. Lisa burst out laughing and stuck her head out of the window as they sheepishly approached the car.

They climbed into the backseat, and she turned around to face them. "Sorry about that, guys," she said, "I couldn't help it. You both looked so keen and cheerful, like you were waiting for the school bus or something."

"Hey, no sweat," said Kierce, picking up a rock-hard, half-eaten burger, loosely wrapped in waxed paper, and dropping it on Jay's lap, "I usually pretend to be a murderous psychopath when I hang out with people for the first time too."

"So what's the plan?" She looked at me expectantly.

"I dunno," I said, shrugging. Deep Cove suddenly seemed more boring than ever. How were we supposed to compete with New York?

"Seriously guys, I'm easy," she said. "What do people do for fun around here? Should we kidnap a tourist or something? C'mon, you guys must do *something* to kill time."

"Not really," Jay said.

"Well," she said, "I guess we could just sit here all night. You guys wanna split that burger back there? It's only a few days old. I might have a deck of cards here somewhere. We could play Crazy Eights."

"Or we could hit up the Spot," said Jay, after a pause.

"She doesn't want to go to the Spot, Jay," said Kierce. "We might as well take her to the dump and get her to fish for old clothes."

"What do you mean, *the Spot*?" she asked.

"It's kind of hard to describe," I said. "It's just this place we go to hang out sometimes."

"We hardly ever go there anymore," said Kierce.

"So do you guys, like, take imaginary girls there and have imaginary sex with them?" she asked. "Hide your Batmobiles? Stuff like that?"

Jay laughed. "It's just a place to chill. There's not much else to do around here, unless you wanna drive in circles all night."

"I'm in, then," said Lisa. "Take me to the Spot."

"All right," said Kierce. "Why the hell not?"

We told Lisa where to drive and got her to park near the path that led onto the tracks. As she got out of the car, she grabbed her bag and then skipped over to us and curtsied.

"Lead the way, guys."

It was a beautiful night, and an almost-full moon lit the old railway tracks. We followed Jay and Kierce through the woods for a while, and then the trees thinned and we were walking along a ledge that looked out past some overgrown fields and a swampy thicket of buckwheat. In the distance, we could make out the thin line of the two-lane highway that moved away from town toward the causeway, the only route off the island. Every so often the concentrated yellow glow of headlights would work its way along the road before disappearing around a bend.

"You don't find this in New York City." Lisa stopped and gestured dramatically, arms stretched wide as she turned in a circle. She said that kind of thing a lot. I felt like asking her if she wanted a list of things that she couldn't find in Deep Cove.

Kierce laughed. "It's just a shitty old road. The tracks aren't even here anymore. It doesn't lead anywhere."

"Does it need to?" she asked.

When we reached the trestle, Kierce went first, reaching back to help Lisa negotiate the steep incline. Jay followed, ready to reach out and grab her if she slipped.

"Guys," she said, "I'm not a china doll. I can handle it."

She scurried easily under the bridge, and we followed her one at a time. Once we were all in the Spot, we jockeyed for space until everyone was comfortable.

The moon cast a million shadows, so everything was either totally clear or completely obscured. Through the cracks of the railway ties above us, we could make out thin lines of stars. Down below, the river burbled past under the shimmering stillness of the leaves on the overhanging trees.

"I can see why you guys come here," Lisa said. "It's impossible to find anyplace this quiet and peaceful in the city."

She rummaged in her bag and pulled out her of skinny cigarettes.

"Anyone mind if I smoke?"

"No, of course not," Kierce lied. Jay pulled a lighter out of his pocket and leaned toward her in one slick motion. Cigarettes were disgusting to me, but I had to envy the smoothness of his gesture.

"So, Lisa," Kierce said, turning toward her and crossing his legs in a ridiculous-looking yoga pose. "Tell us all about yourself."

"Oooh! Am I being interviewed for your club newspaper?" she asked with mock excitement.

"No," he said, "but it's not every day that a beautiful woman like you shows up in boring old Deep Cove and agrees to hang out with a bunch of losers like us. We just want to make the most of it."

She turned to me. "You didn't tell me what a piece of work this guy is."

"Rule Four: Kierce is totally full of shit," I said, earning a shot in the arm from him.

It was weird for us to be hanging out with a girl this way—weird for us to be hanging out with anybody else at the Spot. Lisa fit right in though. Watching the way she and Kierce flirted with each other, I wondered if she wasn't enjoying herself a bit too much.

Eventually it was time to go home, and we climbed back up into the real world. I turned away from the bridge and started walking back along the tracks to the car, but Lisa ran out onto the trestle. Skipping lightly over the inch-wide gaps between the heavy tar-smelling railway ties, she stopped somewhere in the middle, yodeled into the darkness and waited for the echo.

Kierce and Jay both followed her out, but I stayed on solid ground. The trestle was scary enough in the daytime. At night, it was a hundred times more frightening.

So I stood at a safe distance, watching them as they yelled into the emptiness, listening as three distinct voices called out into the night and came spinning back through the darkness as one big echo.

On the way back to the car, Jay and I walked up ahead while Kierce and Lisa lagged behind, chatting and laughing.

"Why the hell didn't you tell Kierce that you have the hots for her?" Jay asked as we listened to them flirting behind us.

I turned around and looked back at them. They definitely seemed to be hitting it off.

I shrugged. "Dunno. It's complicated."

He laughed at me. "Well, it looks like he beat you to it, man. Easy come, easy go, right?"

"THAT WAS FUN!" Lisa said after she dropped them off and we were heading to my place. Kierce had taken forever to get out of the car, making her laugh with one stupid story after another. I'd just sat there trying not to gag.

"Yeah."

"Kierce is funny *and* super cute. I think I'm going to call him. Do you think that's a good idea?"

My heart sank a little. "Yeah, sure. He'd love that."

"Man, you're quiet tonight."

"Sorry," I said. "I'm just exhausted."

"Well, who knows," she said as she pulled into my driveway. "The summer might have just gotten interesting!"

Weren't things interesting enough when it was just the two of us? I got out of the car and walked into my house without turning to wave goodbye.

THIRTEEN

The next morning, my mom knocked on my door to tell me Kierce was on the phone.

"Oh my god, Danny," he said, practically squealing. "She called me! Lisa called me! She asked if I want to do something with her after she gets off work today! Is that a date? I think that's a date!"

"Wow. Great." Just great.

"Man oh man, Dan the man, I owe you big-time. This is so awesome!"

Awesome. Right. I knew it was stupid, but I was jealous.

"So listen, man. Is this going to bother you? Did you like her or something?"

What could I say? *Actually, Kierce, you were right, I'm totally queer. I have no interest in screwing Lisa, but I'd prefer you didn't either, because I saw her first. So back off, or I'll bitch slap you.*

"It's cool, man," I forced myself to say. "I'm not interested. Have at it."

"Awesome, D-man! I'll give you a call tomorrow and fill you in on the details!"

As far as I was concerned, he could keep his details to himself.

That night we had a busy shift, but during a brief lull, Lisa sidled up to me and gave me a hip bump.

"Hey, sexy. Thanks for the good time last night."

"Huh? Oh yeah, sure, no problem."

"Your friends are cool. And the Spot is so great! I want to go back again soon. Maybe we can sneak a bottle of wine from out front. I'll pay for it out of my tips."

"Yeah, sounds good." I kept my head down, concentrating intently on the cheese I was grating.

"So I called Kierce," she said.

"Yeah, I heard." I turned away to grab a bowl from the shelf. "He called me this morning. That's cool."

When I turned back, she was looking at me with her head tilted sideways as if she was trying to figure something out. Before she could say anything, JP called out her order, and she took off to the dining room.

After we closed for the night, I was cleaning up my workstation and she came back to see me again. "So Kierce and I kind of have plans tonight."

"Yeah, no sweat. I'll ask Maisie or Denise to give me a ride home."

"Don't be crazy. I'll totally still drive you. I just won't be able to hang out for long."

I shrugged. "If you really don't mind."

"Of course I don't mind. You know I love hanging out with you after work."

Before driving me home, she drove down the hill to the beach parking lot to have a smoke. I didn't say much, just stared out the car window at the lighthouse in the distance.

"What's bothering you, big guy?" she finally said.

"Nothing."

"C'mon, D. I'm not stupid. You've been ignoring me all day, and now you're acting like the saddest little boy on earth."

"Okay, fine. I just don't understand this thing with Kierce. It just came out of nowhere. What the hell do you see in him anyway?"

She pulled back and looked at me with surprise. "Okay, hold on a minute. What do you mean, what do I see in him? I thought he was one of your best friends."

"He is," I said. "But it's not like you guys have anything in common." *Not like you and me.*

"It's not as if I'm *interested* in him," she said. "It's not like it's some big *thing*, or whatever. I told you last night, I just think he's cool and funny and cute."

"Cute, great."

She turned her head and blew smoke out of the window. "Yeah, cute. I hate to break it to you, Danny, but you're not the only cute guy in Deep Cove. Don't tell me you're jealous."

"What's that supposed to mean?"

"It doesn't mean anything! I just wondered—shit, I don't know—I kind of thought maybe you weren't interested, you know, in girls."

"What?"

"I'm sorry, I just—it felt like—I don't know. I didn't think anything was going to happen between us. But then that night on the hill, I really thought maybe you were going to try to kiss me, and then you didn't, and it got me thinking that you might be gay…"

I stared at her with no idea what to say. My brain scrambled, trying to find the right words. She made it sound so normal, like being gay was just an everyday thing. I felt my heart drop into my stomach, and I had a powerful urge to tell her everything. My brain immediately fought against it, screaming, *No! Tell her she's wrong! Nobody can know!* My brain won.

"Well, you were wrong," I said. I knew I sounded cold and mean, but I didn't care. "Maybe some guys don't think you're very hot. I know I don't. Maybe that's hard for you to believe."

She flinched as if I'd slapped her. "Of course it isn't," she said. "I don't think I'm perfect or anything. I don't understand. I didn't think you'd care about the Kierce thing, I just thought it might be fun…"

"You know what?" I said. "Fuck you, Lisa. I'm not some stupid faggot you can just toy around with, okay?"

Neither of us said anything for a moment. She just sat there staring at me with her mouth hanging open. I got out of the car, slammed the door behind me and ran into the shadows of the sand dunes as fast as I could, dropping to hide behind some tall grass. I heard her car door open. Then she was yelling.

"Danny! Come on! I'm sorry! Really!"

I didn't move. I didn't want her to drive me home, and I didn't want her pity. Most of all, I wanted to be alone. I didn't know why I'd exploded at her. I felt like I was losing my mind.

I was happy that she didn't try to find me. I felt stupid enough already without being chased through the dunes.

Finally, after about ten minutes, I heard her get back into her car and drive away. I backtracked through the dunes to the parking lot, walked up to the road and made my way home. It took me over an hour, and when I finally got there, the lights were out and everyone was asleep.

THE NEXT MORNING, I woke up in a foul, depressed mood. I couldn't believe that Lisa, of all people, was now on the *Danny must be gay* bandwagon. At the same time, I felt like a complete idiot for freaking out at her. I'd been pretty nasty. I doubted she'd ever want to talk to me again. She'd probably tell Kierce everything, and I'd be a laughing stock.

I was lying on the couch wondering if I should just bite the bullet, put together a hobo sack and run away from home, when Alma came in and flopped into the chair next to me.

"Danny, why don't you have a girlfriend?"

What the hell? Had someone formed a committee to harass me? I sat up and looked at her. "Where did that come from?"

"I dunno, I was just wondering if you were sweet on anyone. You know, like Warren Beatty and Natalie Wood in *Splendor in the Grass*. Although hopefully not *totally* like that, because Natalie Wood's character went bonkers. Besides, you aren't nearly as handsome as Warren Beatty."

"Gee, thanks."

"Hey, don't take it personally. Warren Beatty was a total hottie. So why don't you? Have a girlfriend, that is."

I closed my eyes and made a face. I wished I had a real answer for that one.

"I dunno, Al. I guess I haven't found the right girl yet."

"Huh. Well, don't you think you should be looking? You're not getting any younger."

"Alma! I'm only seventeen. Why does it matter?"

"I told you, I was just thinking about it. Anyway, I think I might have some ideas about what kind of girl you should go out with."

"Oh yeah? Fill me in." At this point, I was willing to take love lessons from anyone.

She chewed on her bottom lip. "Well, she'd probably have kind of a Rita Hayworth thing going on. Thick red hair, pale skin."

"Okay," I said. "Sounds good. What else?"

"Well, she'd probably dress kind of like Annie Hall."

"That sounds like a decent combo," I said.

"You think so? Because I'm pretty sure she just pulled into the driveway in Chitty Chitty Bang Bang."

I jumped up and looked out the window. Sure enough, Old Bessie was parked in the driveway, and Lisa was sitting behind the wheel.

"Alma! How long has she been out there?"

"Just a few minutes."

"Thanks a lot for telling me." I headed to the front door and turned around before going outside. "By the way, she's not my girlfriend."

"Well, you never know. 'This could be the start of a beautiful friendship.'"

I walked up to Old Bessie and knocked on the window. I half expected that Lisa had come just to tell me off, so I was relieved when she smiled up at me and pointed to the seat next to her. I got into the car.

"Hey," I said.

"Listen, D," she said, talking fast. "I know I hurt your feelings last night, and I'd feel really bad if we couldn't still be friends and I'm really sorry and can we please just forget that it ever happened?

"You didn't hurt my feelings," I lied. "You just kind of took me by surprise."

"Well, if I—I don't know—offended your manhood, or anything like that, I didn't mean to insinuate anything. It was stupid of me."

I didn't say anything. She reached over and put her hand on my arm, and I looked at her reluctantly. She pulled her sunglasses down her nose so I could see her eyes. She looked really sincere, which made me feel even worse about freaking out at her.

"Can we please be friends again?" she said. "I don't know what I'd do if I had to spend the rest of the summer not hanging out with you."

"You don't have to apologize," I said. "I was a total asshole. It's just that you aren't the first person who's said that to me recently—about being gay. I'm pretty sick of it."

"Hey, I totally get it. I shouldn't have been so quick to jump to conclusions. Listen, let's start fresh and pretend that last night never happened."

I nodded. "Sounds good."

"Awesome!" she said. "Now that we're best friends again, I have a great idea. Why don't we make it our mission for the rest of the summer to find you an awesome girl?"

"Sure," I said, trying to sound enthusiastic, but wishing I had the balls to tell her the truth.

"You know," she said, "you really don't have to worry about me not hanging out with you anymore. This Kierce thing—it's just a summer fling."

FOURTEEN

"If you know how to cook, you will never go hungry,"
JP said, "and you will always have work, wherever you go.
The world needs chefs like it needs carpenters. Govern-
ments might collapse, and aliens might invade, but people
will always want to eat good food."

He turned to the stove and flicked on a burner,
grabbed some olive oil and swirled it into a pan, and
followed it up with some garlic.

"If we had fresh chilis, I'd use those, but we don't,
so we'll improvise. Get me that red bottle on that shelf
over there," he directed. I grabbed the plastic squeeze
bottle and passed it to him. He held it up and showed
me the label, a rooster surrounded by Asian characters.

"Sriracha sauce," he said. "Chilis, vinegar, garlic and salt. Delicious. Every kitchen needs some. Good on eggs, good in a marinade, you name it. But today, we make pasta *aglio e olio*."

Sree rotcha sauce. Pasta ally-oh ee oh-lee-oh. I was getting used to hearing lots of names for things that I doubted I'd remember, let alone be able to spell.

He squeezed some of the sauce into the pan. Then he reached into the fridge for a container full of linguine that I'd cooked and oiled that morning, grabbed a handful and tossed it in the pan. He poured in some more oil, shook it all around and slid it onto two small plates. Then he finished them with some cheese and handed one to me.

"Mmm," I said, my mouth full. "Spicy. Good."

"About fifty cents a plate. Another reason a cook never goes hungry. If you know what you're doing, you can make delicious food for very little money. Even a chef without two dimes to rub together can eat well, always."

I was still spending a lot of time chopping and peeling, but JP had been teaching me more stuff every day. He'd gradually introduced me to actual cooking by letting me try my hand at pasta.

"There are two things to remember when cooking pasta," he said. "The water should be as salty as the sea, and you must never overcook it. It should be *al dente*. Firm, not hard. The mouth should feel it, should need to chew it."

Every couple of days, he'd teach me something new. He showed me how to make a medium-poached egg, his idea of the perfect food. We made pastry, chilling the ingredients first and then working quickly so the end result would be flaky and light. We picked fresh herbs from the pots he'd planted out back, and he showed me which ones to use with which foods. One day, we butchered a side of beef into various steaks and roasts, and then roasted the leftover bits and bones and made a rich stock.

But it was when he began to demonstrate sauces that I finally fell completely in love with cooking. I had a hard time believing that there were so many thousands of ways to complement food with pan reductions and vinaigrettes and marinades. I slowly whisked lemon juice into butter and egg yolks, and stirred in fragrant chopped dill for smooth, rich hollandaise sauce. Fresh figs and balsamic vinegar, cooked over very low heat for a long time, created a sweet and tart syrup that could be drizzled over goat cheese and fresh greens, or pooled underneath golden-seared scallops. I opened cans of Italian plum tomatoes and crushed them up with my hands, threw them into a pot with some sautéed onion and garlic, and let the whole mess simmer with a handful of fresh basil and oregano for marinara sauce that I imagined smelled and tasted like the Italian countryside.

Cooking created endless possibilities. I began to realize that you could travel the world without leaving your kitchen.

It was the first time I had ever been really good at something. JP told me that I was a natural, and I actually believed him. The more he showed me, the more I wanted to learn. As I watched him confidently throw down dozens of perfectly cooked plates during one busy shift after another, it began to dawn on me that I could picture myself in his shoes. I belonged in the kitchen.

"How did you become a chef?" I asked JP one day when he was showing me how to make a compound butter by mashing cheese, herbs and butter into a paste and rolling it in plastic wrap.

"I did it the hard way," he said. "I started off where you are. *Lower* than where you are, and I worked my way up through the kitchen. I couldn't afford to go to school, so I had to pay my dues in the trenches."

"There are schools?"

"Sure. These days there are lots of them. In my opinion, the best one in the country is in Montreal. The Atwater

Culinary Institute. They have some great teachers." He stopped what he was doing and looked at me. "Have you been thinking about becoming a chef?"

I imagined living in a city like Montreal, wearing a beret and a striped scarf and biking through the old city to a school full of cute guys with French accents. There was bound to be an endless supply of exotic groceries, not to mention hundreds of fantastic restaurants where I could work to pay my way through school.

"Yeah," I said. "I've been thinking that I might want to be a chef. Like you."

"*Comme moi?* Very flattering, Danny. But you should know that there's a lot more to cooking than what we're doing here. It's a tough business, and there will be days, mark my words, when the look of food, even the most delicious food in the world, will make you sick."

"I still feel like it could be the right thing for me."

"Well, in that case, I'd be honored to help you any way I can." He reached up to his neatly shelved row of cookbooks, pulled down a thick, serious-looking book and dropped it with a thud on the counter next to me. "You can start with this. Take it home and read it."

The book, *Mastering the Art of French Cooking*, was dog-eared and had food stains on every page. Inside, I found hundreds of elaborate recipes that sounded as if they'd take days to make. I started reading it at home in the mornings before work, and on the beach with Lisa and the guys. The more I learned, the more I wanted to know, and my resolve to become a chef became stronger every day.

For the first time, I felt excited about my future. Cooking was the escape route I'd been looking for. JP had lived and worked all over the world. I could do that too. Deep Cove would be a place I just dropped into once in a while. My real life was somewhere else, waiting for me.

THE DAY MY DAD flew home, Mom and Alma and I went to the airport to pick him up. He dropped his bags as he came out of the gate and picked my mom up off her feet, twirling her around. Then he put her down and gave her a huge kiss on the mouth.

"'Fasten your seatbelts,'" Alma said to me. "'It's gonna be a bumpy night.'"

Dad bent over and gave her a big bear hug and then reached out to give me a manly handshake.

"There he is," he said. "The working man himself."

"So is there any news with the contractor?" my mom asked him as we were driving home.

"What kind of news?" he asked.

"I don't know. Maybe there are some new opportunities coming up."

He sighed, then forced a smile. "Do you know what, Mary? I just got home, and that's about the last thing I want to talk about right now." My mom didn't say anything; she just smiled tensely and turned to look out the side window.

"What are you most excited to do now that you're home, Dad?" Alma asked him.

"Do you know what, Alma? I can't wait to just kick back and put my feet up."

IT SEEMED LIKE that's *all* he wanted to do. Usually when Dad came home from Alberta, he acted like he was making up for lost time. He'd start new building projects around the house, or bug me and Alma to go fishing with him. This time, though, he seemed content to sit on the deck and struggle with the crossword or just stare out at the garden for hours on end.

Weirdest of all, he didn't once bring up university with me. He asked me vague questions about my friends and took a quick look at my report card, but there was no sign of his usual obsession with my future.

One morning, a few days after he arrived, I came into the kitchen and found Mom standing at the counter.

She was nursing a cup of tea and staring out the window at the back of Dad's head.

"Is it my imagination, or has he been acting strange?" she asked me.

"Totally strange," I said. I remembered Lisa's story about her mom. Was that happening to Dad? "Do you think he's going crazy?" I asked her.

She laughed. "Crazy like a fox, maybe." She rinsed out her cup and sighed. "Who knows. I think the whole Alberta thing is starting to get to him. I've never seen him this bothered about getting laid off. He doesn't want to talk about it at all."

"It's not like this is the first time it's happened," I said.

"Well, that might be the problem. The money's good out there, but it's a tough life. Tough on all of us, but especially on him. Why do you think he's always giving you advice about universities and stuff?"

"I guess so," I said, "but he hasn't even tried to talk about that stuff with me since he got home. Not that I'm complaining."

"Well, you never know. Maybe he's so frustrated about his own career that he isn't in the mood to talk to you about yours."

It had never occurred to me that Dad ever got discouraged about anything. He always sounded so sure of how

I should live my life that it came as a bit of a surprise to hear that he might be unhappy with his own.

I wanted to talk to Dad about my plan to go to culinary school. If he realized that I'd finally found my calling, it might cheer him up a little bit, but I needed to make sure he was in a good mood when I brought it up. I decided to wait for the perfect opportunity.

As it turned out, Mom had her own plans to cheer Dad up. On my next day off, she announced that we were going to have a family night. She and Alma drove into town and came home with a pizza and a bunch of chips and chocolate bars. We ate supper in the living room and watched *Vertigo*—Alma's suggestion. I looked over at Mom and Dad sitting on the couch with their arms around each other, and at Alma, sitting cross-legged on the floor, her eyes glued to the TV. They all looked so content, it made me sad to think that I might never have children of my own. That I'd have to hide the real me from the people who knew me best.

I knew my days in Deep Cove were numbered. Now that I had a plan, I told myself that if I could just make it through one more school year, if I could just keep pretending to be someone I wasn't, then I could move away for cooking school and start living my life. Maybe in Montreal I could finally be myself.

FIFTEEN

"I think I'm in love with her," said Kierce.

I looked over at him, and I could tell from the bizarre dreamy look on his face that he was telling the truth. Or at least what he thought was the truth.

We were in his van, wishing there was something more fun to do than just cruise the strip. Tonight was the first time since he and Lisa had hooked up that it was just me and the guys hanging out. Lisa had rushed away after work, saying something about having promised to spend the evening with her aunt.

"Bullshit," said Jay. "You just love getting laid."

"No way, man. When you know, you know."

"What happened to the rules?" I asked him. "You know, Rule Forty-five: Love 'em and leave 'em. Or Rule Eighty-one: Women—can't live with 'em, can't live with 'em."

He waved his hand at me, brushing away my comments. "You guys haven't experienced the joys of true love. When you do, you'll understand that there's really only one Golden Rule: All you need is love."

"Excuse me," said Jay. "I'm gonna go barf for a few minutes."

The Lisa and Kierce thing hadn't been as big a deal as I'd thought it would be. Instead of disappearing into some kind of couple's bubble, they spent most of their time with me and Jay. I was happy to be hanging out with the guys again, but I worried Kierce was setting himself up for a big disappointment. "A summer fling." That's what Lisa had called it. That definitely didn't line up with all his love talk.

"What makes you think you're in love?" I asked him. "You've only been dating for a couple of weeks."

"You just know, Dan. It's a feeling you get when your heart and your wang are in perfect harmony."

"Lovely," I said.

"Oh yeah!" said Jay. "That reminds me! I was at the Spot yesterday, and you horndogs are so busted!"

"What do you mean?" asked Kierce.

"Don't play dumb," said Jay. "You forgot to remove the evidence."

Kierce gave him a blank look. "I don't know what you're talking about."

"The condom wrapper? You forgot to remove your garbage after your love session."

"Gross," I said.

"No way," said Kierce. "We never did it at the Spot. We haven't even gone back there since the night our true love first bloomed."

"I guess it was just a matter of time before someone found the place," said Jay.

"Yeah," I said, "but it's pretty disgusting to think about people doing it at the Spot."

"I don't think it's disgusting," said Kierce. "I think it's awesome. I wish I'd thought of it first."

LISA BREEZED INTO the kitchen the next day and rummaged around in her purse before thrusting a piece of paper at me. "Look!" she said.

I unfolded the paper, which had obviously been ripped from a telephone pole.

WONDERFUL WALLBURN'S ROLLING CARNIVAL
Rides! Games! Concessions! August 11–13

"It'll be fun!" she said. "Something to do besides driving in circles."

It wasn't exactly my idea of a good time. Every summer for as long as I could remember, Wallburn's Carnival had set up in a field outside of town. It was a rip-off, but Lisa had a point—it could be fun to do something different.

"I'M NOT A BIG FAN of these things," said Kierce a couple of nights later as we tried to find a place to park in the field. "Everyone knows carnies are a bunch of queers. I don't like having to walk around watching my back."

Lisa turned and looked at him with her mouth hanging open.

"Are you kidding me? Queers? What is this, the Middle Ages?"

"Who cares? I don't like fruits. Or—what?— am I supposed to say 'homosexuals'?" he asked. "What's the big deal?"

"Big deal? Oh, I don't know, except that some of my best friends are gay. Not to mention Denise."

My heart skipped a beat. Denise was gay? I remembered what my mom had said about Denise leaving Deep Cove because of gossip, and not getting along with her parents. Why on earth had she moved back to Deep Cove?

The four of us got out of the van in an uncomfortable silence and paid for tickets at the front gate. Kierce tried to pay for Lisa, but she shot him the evil eye. "Not a chance, hillbilly."

The carnival was pretty crappy: a few rusted-out rides and a row of games with cheap prizes hanging on pegboards behind them. Almost right away, we ran into Maisie and her friend Diana.

"Oh my god, I'm so excited to see you guys!" Maisie said. She looked right at me and smiled broadly. "I was hoping you'd be here!"

"Come on," said Lisa, grabbing me by the hand and pulling me away into the crowd.

"What's going on?" I asked, glancing back over my shoulder and shrugging apologetically at Maisie.

"I need to get away from Kierce for a few minutes, before I hit him or something."

She dragged me into the lineup for the Ferris wheel, and a scruffy guy in his early twenties with bloodshot eyes grabbed our tickets and snapped us into a seat. I wondered if it was true what Kierce said about carnies being gay. I discreetly checked the guy out and decided that running away to join the circus probably wasn't the thing for me. A few minutes later we lifted off. As the ride lurched into the air, its tinny music competed with the unsettling sound of metal grinding against metal. I did my best to ignore it.

"He's driving me crazy," Lisa said, pointing down into the crowd. I looked and saw Maisie cheerfully talking Jay's ear off as they boarded the Whirl-A-Gig. They were followed closely by Diana and Kierce, who looked miserable.

"Wow, you sure are in a crappy mood, aren't you?" I said.

"I know, I know." She looked at me and forced a smile to her face. "Things at home totally suck. My mom is coming to stay with me at Cheryl's house."

"No way!" I said.

"Yeah, well, what can you do? Anyway, every time she calls, she talks about how excited she is to come spend the rest of the summer with me, and if I'm not totally enthusiastic about it, she pulls a major guilt trip. Now, to top it all off, Kierce is turning out to be such an asshole."

"He's not really, he just says stupid crap." I didn't know why I was defending him. I hated the stuff he said as much as she did.

"It's not even that," she said. "I'm just finding him really annoying. He wants to spend every free minute with me. It's getting old fast."

"Why don't you end it then?" I asked her.

"Too much effort. Besides, he's not *totally* useless, if you catch my drift."

"Okay, great, too much information," I said. It wasn't fair for her to string him along like that, but I figured that part of it had to be his own fault. Besides, I couldn't help feeling a bit of mean-spirited satisfaction that things weren't working out for him the way he wanted them to. Maybe it would be good for Kierce to realize that the world didn't always play by his rules.

When we met up with the group again, he immediately apologized to Lisa.

"I'm sorry," he said. "I don't know why I had to shoot my mouth off like that."

"He really is sorry," said Maisie. "He talked about it the whole time we were on the ride."

"Don't worry about it," said Lisa, not bothering to look him in the eye. She still sounded pissed off, but by the time we'd all grabbed something to eat from the concession stand and found an empty picnic table, she had returned to her old self. When she told us a funny story about getting stuck in a changing room at Macy's department store, Kierce laughed harder than the rest of us put together.

Eventually, we decided to call it a night. "So I'll see you at work tomorrow, right?" Maisie asked me as I got into Kierce's van.

"You got it," I replied.

"Awesome!" she said. "I'll see you there. Bye, guys!" She hurried away to her own car, Diana close behind.

As soon as we were on the road, Jay reached over and poked me in the arm, repeatedly. "Oooooh, Danny Boy, looks like you might finish up this summer with a bang after all."

"Quit it!" I swatted him away. "What the hell are you talking about?"

"Oh, come on, Danno," said Kierce, rolling his eyes at me in the rearview mirror. "She's obviously into you." Lisa and Jay both nodded.

"Who, Maisie? I didn't notice anything. You guys are crazy."

"Oh my god, I'm soooooo super happy you came to the carnival, Dannypoo!" said Lisa.

"If you think she's so stupid," I asked her, "why are you pushing this?"

"I'm not suggesting that *I* sleep with her, I'm suggesting that *you* sleep with her. What I think of her is beside the point, and you've told me you like her just fine."

"I do like her," I said. "She's really nice and easygoing."

"She's also hot, Dan," said Kierce. "So what are you waiting for? Remember the Golden Rule, my man."

I looked at Jay, who said, "It's up to you, man, but I'd say that she definitely likes you. She kept talking about you. She says you're 'super-duper nice.'"

"I'm not sure I like her that way," I managed to squeeze out.

"I understand if you don't want to date her," said Lisa. "She's as dumb as a brick. But you could definitely get into her pants if you wanted to."

"Wow, that's classy."

"Oh, for crying out loud, Danny, why do you have to be such a romantic?" she said. "Think with your dick for a change!"

"You sound like Kierce," I told her.

"Rule Thirty-two million: Boobs and sex and girls and panties and sex. When in doubt, listen to the brain in your pants. Go team," she said, in a surprisingly good imitation of Kierce.

"You got that right!" he said, reaching over to grab her hand. She snatched it away.

"Don't get any ideas. I'm still pissed off at you, homophobe." She turned back to me. "Danny! Everything doesn't have to be some big huge *thing*. You're seventeen. Nobody expects you to get married and have a baby. You should be trying to get laid, and if Strawberry Shortcake there is the best option, then you should take advantage of it."

"Yeah, we'll see," was all I said. I was glad when they finally dropped me off at home. I'd had enough of all three of them.

SIXTEEN

"Um, I was wondering," said Maisie, "if I could maybe hang out with you guys sometime after work."

We were finishing our shift a couple of nights after the carnival, and Lisa and I were getting ready to leave.

"Yeah, for sure," Lisa said. "If you don't mind driving around with a bunch of fools. What are you doing now?"

"Really? Nothing! I don't have any plans! Let me just grab my purse!"

Maisie bounced away happily.

"What was that all about?" I asked.

Lisa raised her eyebrows at me. "She wants ya, tiger," she said. "Who am I to stand in the way of true love?"

We'd made plans to meet the guys on Main Street. We eventually spotted them huddled with a group of people in the small park in the middle of town. Lisa pulled up by the sidewalk and pressed on the horn.

In a few seconds, Jay and Kierce came running across the park and up to the car. They did a double take when they saw Maisie, who waved cheerfully and scooched into the middle of the backseat to give them both room. Kierce immediately reached around the seat and poked me in the arm. I turned and gave him a dirty look, but he just grinned at me.

Before their doors were even closed, Lisa burned rubber. Old Bessie shuddered, and something behind the dash began to clink as Lisa pushed the car to the brink of its power. An awful-smelling smoke wafted from the vents.

"If this car blows up, it's been nice knowing you guys," Lisa said. "But we don't have time to worry about that. We're on a mission." The car chugged along toward the outskirts of town, and she threw her bag onto my lap. "There's a tape in there with a baby-blue label. It has *Bitches Don't Quit* written on it in pink ink." She turned to the backseat. "That's my girl Naomi's motto."

"I love it!" squealed Maisie.

I flipped quickly through a pile of tapes and came up with the one she wanted.

"Side B, please. Rewind to beginning. Press *Play*. Thank you, co-pilot, that will be all."

"Hey!" whined Kierce. "I should get to be the co-pilot. You're my little woman, after all."

"I really wish you'd stop talking about me like that," said Lisa. She didn't sound like she was joking. She seemed to have less patience with Kierce each time I saw them together.

The tape crackled on, and Lisa cranked the volume. "Highway to Hell" reverberated through the car as she pressed on the gas and we accelerated into the night.

"Where are you taking us?" asked Jay.

"Patience, soldiers."

"You guys are awesome!" Maisie exclaimed.

Lisa chugged along the empty two-lane highway for a few miles and then, without warning, cut the wheel and spun onto an almost hidden gravel road. Without slowing down, she barreled over the potholes and ruts in the overgrown road. Tree branches popped in and out of the open windows, scratching at our hair, but she kept gunning along before finally coming to an abrupt stop in front of an abandoned farmhouse.

"Wow," said Kierce, "I should have worn a diaper."

"Where are we?" I asked, but Lisa didn't answer. She just grabbed her bag and got out of the car. Reluctantly we followed her into the darkness.

"Are you going to kill us dead, Lisa?" Kierce asked.

"Wait a minute," Jay said. "I know this place. My uncle took me here a few times when I was a kid. There's a little lake behind that house. We used to come here to go swimming."

"Ladies and gentlemen, we have a winner!" said Lisa. "Come on, it shouldn't be far." She took off behind the house, Jay and Maisie close behind her. Kierce and I exchanged wary glances, and then followed them.

"Man," Kierce whispered to me, "this is totally your chance. Don't blow it!"

I ignored him.

Just as Jay had said, there was a small calm lake surrounded by trees and reflecting the bright night sky. Lisa followed a path through the weeds, and then sat on the edge of the bank and began removing her shoes.

"How did you find out about this place?" I asked.

"Denise told me about it. When I mentioned that I wanted to go swimming in a lake for a change, she said that when she was in high school, she and her friends would come here and get drunk and go skinny dipping."

"*Hello!*" said Kierce.

"Not so fast, big guy, I'm gonna keep my underwear on, and if you don't want me to leave you here, you should keep yours on too. So who's coming in?"

WAY TO GO

"I am!" To my surprise, Maisie couldn't get her jeans and T-shirt off fast enough. She ran to the edge of the bank and did a cannonball into the water.

"It's beautiful!" she yelled.

Lisa and the guys stripped to their underwear and followed Maisie in.

"Drop your pants, Disco Dan!" yelled Kierce.

"I'm good," I said. "I'm just going to stay here."

"If you don't get in, I'm going to jump up on that bank and push you in, clothes and all."

"Fine, fine." I slowly stripped down to my boxers and sat on the bank, letting my feet slip into the water first. It was surprisingly warm compared to the ocean, and I was about to slide the rest of the way in when Jay jumped out and yanked me by the legs into the water. I rose, choking and splashing, to the sight of the four of them laughing at me.

It was a beautiful night, and we floated around, occasionally splashing each other, but mostly just lying on our backs and looking up at the stars and talking.

Maisie turned out to be more interesting—and smarter—than any of us had given her credit for. Apparently, she wanted to change the world. She told us that it was her dream to go to medical school and work in Africa, treating kids with AIDS.

"We don't know how bad some people have it," she said. "Imagine growing up without a mom, in that kind of poverty, knowing that you were going to die."

"It would suck," said Kierce.

"Yes, Kierce, it would probably suck," said Lisa sarcastically.

"You know what I mean."

"You guys are getting awful heavy," said Jay.

"My fault, sorry!" Maisie said. "I have an idea!" She swam over to the edge of the lake and climbed out of the water. She shook out her hair, and water streamed over the goose bumps that popped up on her legs. Her wet bra was practically transparent, and I knew that the other guys were getting an eyeful. I turned away, and Kierce caught my eye, shaking his head at me, disappointed.

"Let's play truth or dare!" Maisie hollered.

Kierce and Jay groaned along with me, but Lisa yelled, "Come on guys, it'll be fun! I'll go first. Truth!"

"Awesome!" Maisie said. She thought for a moment and then said, "What's the most embarrassing thing about your family?"

I cringed, but Lisa didn't seem fazed. She swam over and climbed up to join Maisie on the bank.

"Embarrassing? That's an easy one! How's this? My mom is a nutbar. Nervous breakdowns, suicide attempts, the whole bullshit thing. My dad couldn't handle her so he took off, and I came here for the summer to—I don't know—get some *space* from it all."

I couldn't look at her. The whole thing was really awkward, and I wondered what she was trying to prove. Maisie stood next to Lisa, looking uncomfortable. Nobody knew what to say, and then Lisa finally broke the silence.

"But guess what?" she said. "She followed me here, and now she sits in my aunt's house all day, with the curtains closed, smoking cigarettes and staring at the wall."

I glanced at Kierce. I could tell from his confused expression that Lisa hadn't bothered to tell him about her mom.

"Don't worry, kids," Lisa said. "We've all got problems, so whatcha gonna do?" With that, she took a flying leap and cannonballed into the lake, right in the middle of where the rest of us were treading water.

"Your turn, Dan!" Jay yelled. I could tell he was trying to change the subject. "Truth or dare?"

Everyone turned to look at me, and my heart started pounding. I plugged my nose and let myself slowly sink underwater. After a few seconds I surfaced and took a breath. "Dare, I guess."

"I got one!" yelled Kierce. "I dare you to swim over to Maisie and make out with her in front of us."

"Yes!" yelled Lisa.

143

I wanted to sink back under and not come up. "Come on, Kierce," I said, "don't be a moron." I didn't dare look in Maisie's direction.

"What do you mean? It's truth or dare. Do you want me to dare you to say a bad word? Don't be such a chicken-shit. You don't mind, do you, Maisie?"

She didn't say anything. I glanced up to where she was still standing on the bank, and saw that she'd crossed her arms over her chest and was looking at the ground, obviously embarrassed.

"You're such an asshole, Kierce," I said, awkwardly paddling to the edge of the lake. I crawled out, grabbed my clothes and walked back up the pathway toward the car.

"Come on, Danny, act your age, for Christ's sake," he yelled after me.

"Speak for yourself, dick!" I hollered back.

I pulled on my shorts and then sat down on the front step of the old house. After a few minutes, Maisie came up the path and sat down next to me. I was glad that she'd put her T-shirt back on.

"You okay?" she asked.

"Yeah, sorry about that."

"Hey, don't apologize. That was super awkward! At least you didn't have to stand there in front of everyone in your wet underwear!"

We both laughed.

"I don't know why he has to be such an asshole all the time," I said.

"Yeah, well, maybe he thought he was doing you a favor," she said.

I stayed quiet. I wasn't sure I liked where this was going.

"I was thinking," she said, after a pause, "maybe sometime you and I could, I don't know, hang out, after work or something..."

"Sure," I said. "You should start hanging out with us more."

"I kind of meant just the two of us, like a date"—she laughed nervously—"or as much of one as you can have in Deep Cove."

"Maisie," I said, feeling like the biggest jerk on the planet, "I really like you, but—"

Before I could finish, she jumped up and said, "That's okay. It was kind of a stupid idea...I just thought...you know...you never know."

"Hey!" I said, reaching up and grabbing her by the hand to pull her back down next to me. "Seriously, I think you're awesome. I just really don't think I want a girl-friend right now."

She looked me in the eye. "You like Lisa, don't you?"

"No, it's not that."

"It's okay, I won't say anything to Kierce. I totally understand. Anyway, it's no big deal. At least it'll be nice to not feel awkward around you at work anymore."

"You were feeling awkward?"

"Totally! For like, weeks now! I can't believe you didn't notice. I talk a lot when I'm nervous."

"I'm kind of dense like that."

She stood up again. "Seriously, no big deal, let's pretend I didn't say anything." She turned and looked back down the path. "Let's go see if those guys are ready to go home."

When we were back at the car, Kierce told Maisie to take the front seat. He grabbed my arm and pulled me into the backseat with Jay. "I was trying to do you a favor," he whispered.

"I get it," I told him, "but why don't you let me take care of myself from now on."

SEVENTEEN

The next morning, I was playing checkers with Alma when my dad came in from the garden.

"Kierce is out in the driveway," he said. "Were you expecting him?"

"No."

When I walked outside, Kierce rolled his window down. "Can you come for a quick drive with me?"

"Uh, sure, I guess so."

As soon as we pulled out of the driveway, he started talking really fast. "My mom told me *an hour ago* that I have to go to Ontario with her *tomorrow morning,* and Lisa isn't answering my calls, and I just want to see her before I go because I'm worried that she's going to ditch me while I'm out of town, and I almost wish I had a job so I didn't have to go, because Rule Ninety-seven: When the cat's away, the mouse will play, and I never thought that I'd be the cat!"

"Okay, take it easy," I said. "What are you talking about?"

"Just what I said! I have to leave town tomorrow morning—something about going to see my grandparents. My mom says it's an emergency, but she won't tell me what it's about, and Lisa's been acting really weird, and I'm worried that this is going to be the last nail in the coffin!"

"I thought you guys were, like, casual."

"Well yeah, we are. I guess. But I'm totally into her, I mean I *really* like her, Danny! You know that! *She* must know that!"

"Well, maybe you've been acting a little bit too serious for her."

"Why? Did she say something?"

"No," I lied. "I don't talk to her about you guys. I could care less, and it's none of my business anyway."

"I don't know what to think. She's the one who called me and asked me out! New Golden Rule: Girls are crazy!"

"Maybe she's just preoccupied now that her mom is here," I said. I knew there was more to it than that, but the guy was frantic. I didn't want to push him off the deep end.

"That's another thing! She didn't tell me *any* of that stuff about her mom! We've been going out for weeks, and not a word! Then she just unloads it on everyone at the lake, as if it's no big deal."

"Well, we *were* playing truth or dare."

"Whatever. Anyway, we're leaving tomorrow morning, and I don't know what to do!" He smacked his hand onto the steering wheel.

"Kierce, you do realize that Lisa's going to be leaving town for good in a few weeks, don't you?"

"Yeah, but I figured if I could make her like me as much as I like her, that we could commute or something."

"Okay, come on, Kierce, get a grip. That's the stupidest thing I ever heard."

"Yeah, maybe. But I figured that we'd at least enjoy the summer together! I'm telling you, man, I really like her. I know it sounds crazy, but I really do."

He looked miserable. I wasn't used to Kierce asking for advice. He was usually way too busy dishing it out.

"I don't know what to tell you, man," I said. "Just try to have a good trip."

"Easy for you to say. You've never met my grand-parents. They're, like, mean old trolls, and their house smells like cats and cheese. Listen, Danny, you have to promise me you'll tell me if anything happens."

"What do you mean?"

"You know, if she says anything about me, or whatever. Just call me at my grandparents' house."

"Okay," I said.

"Thanks, man. I knew I could count on you."

WHEN I MENTIONED Kierce's trip to Lisa at work later that day, all she said was, "So what? It doesn't really matter. I told you, it's not like we're a couple. We were just having some fun for the summer."

"But you still like him, right?"

"Sure, I like him fine," she said, helping me scrape plates into the garbage, "but it's not like he's my type. That was kind of the attraction, I guess. He's cute, but he's sort of a dork, and he's funny, and he's a bit of a redneck—totally different from the guys I date back home. But I'd never in a million years be with somebody like him in my real life."

"Well, I don't think he feels the same way, Lisa. I think he really likes you."

"Yeah, no kidding. The other day he actually mentioned coming to visit me in New York in the fall.

Can you believe that?" She sighed. "This whole thing was a bad idea. I never would have guessed that he'd get all crazy lovey-dovey on me. It's probably a good thing he's leaving town. This just takes care of the problem."

Maybe for you, I thought.

"Well I think you should at least tell him how you feel," I said.

"Oh god, why does this have to be such a big deal?"

"Come on, Lisa, it's only fair," I said.

"Fine, I'll talk to him when he comes back from Ontario." But I wondered if she would. She sure didn't sound very concerned.

I KIND OF EXPECTED that with Kierce out of the picture, I'd get to spend more time with Lisa, but it didn't really work out that way. The night after he left, she told me that she couldn't drive me home. She said that there was something going on with her mom, but she didn't elaborate. Denise offered to give me a lift instead.

"So how are you liking your new gig?" she asked once we were in her truck.

"I love it," I said. "JP's teaching me so much."

She laughed. "Trust me, he's just happy to have someone who's willing to listen to him. I try not to, if I can help it. Anyway, the restaurant is busier than I ever expected, so it's great for him to have the extra help."

"So you're happy with the way things are going?" I asked.

"Oh yeah. If you'd told me ten years ago that I'd be living in Deep Cove again, running my own place, I'd have laughed at you. Now I have a hard time believing I ever left."

"Why *did* you leave?"

She turned and looked at me and then thought for a few seconds before answering.

"Well, you know I'm gay, right?"

I nodded.

"Well, that wasn't the easiest thing in a town like Deep Cove, believe me," she said. "It was extra hard because I couldn't even really hide it. I was pretty butch from the get-go." She chuckled. "I was the kind of girl who wanted to play hockey with the boys, and back in the late seventies that kind of thing just didn't happen."

"You didn't—you know—have any doubts about it?"

"About being gay? Well sure, a little bit. I tried to go on dates with guys in high school. Total disasters, every last one, but by the time I graduated, I pretty much knew. I figured I could pretend all I wanted, but eventually I was just gonna have to be me. Sounds cheesy, but that's how it happened.

"Long story short, I felt that my only option was to get out of town. I didn't think that I could tell anyone in Deep Cove who I was, and I wanted to go out and meet the perfect woman, so I hit the road as soon as I got my diploma. Lived in Vancouver, spent some time in New York, and then I ended up in Montreal, and that's where I met Danielle."

"Danielle?"

"Danielle was my partner for almost ten years. We split up last year."

She looked out the window and didn't say anything for a few moments.

"Anyway," she continued, "as you know, when my mom died, I came home to take care of things. It was a good excuse to leave Montreal for a few weeks. Then while I was here, taking care of all that bullshit, I remembered what I love about the place. The people are great, the landscape is beautiful. The air smells clean and fresh. I heard about the Burger Shack going on the market so I decided, spur of the moment, that I wanted to move home."

"Are you happy you did it?"

"Yep. The only thing I really regret is that my parents were both dead by the time I moved home. I never got to spend much time with them as an adult. I was just a kid when I left, and I never gave them much credit. With the gay stuff, I mean.

"I came home every couple of years for Christmas, or for a few days in the summer once in a while, but I never had the balls to tell them the truth, let alone bring Danielle home with me. Maybe they knew all along. I guess I'll never know."

"It must still be pretty hard though," I said. "Being gay, I mean."

"Well, you'd be surprised. There are a lot of ignorant people in the world, but if you can learn to ignore them, then all kinds of other fantastic people start popping up in your life. And some people just end up surprising you. I wish I'd given my folks the chance to know the real me. Instead, I was so scared that I shut everyone out and ran away. That's no way to go through life."

"Yeah, I think I know what you mean," I said.

"Oh yeah?"

"Well, not exactly," I hastened to explain, "but I've been thinking I might want to become a chef, and I don't know how to tell my parents."

"No shit, eh? A chef?"

"Well, I'm not sure, but I really like helping JP out in the kitchen, and—I don't know, I've never really been able to imagine what I was going to do with my life.

But now I keep thinking about maybe going to culinary school."

She pulled into my driveway.

"If you don't mind," I said as I got out of the truck, "could you not say anything to anyone about the chef thing? I haven't figured out the best way to tell my folks about it."

"Maybe you don't need to tell them," she said. "Maybe you should show them instead."

"What do you mean?"

"Cook for them. Let the food do the talking."

EIGHTEEN

The next afternoon when I showed up for work, JP gave me a funny smile and then hurried out of the kitchen without saying anything. I was putting on my apron when I noticed the envelope sitting in the middle of my workspace. It was thick and official-looking, with an embossed gold seal on the upper corner. *Atwater Culinary Institute*, it said in letters that curved around a stylized knife and chef's hat.

I shoved it in my backpack and waited until I got home to look at it. I flipped through glossy photos of an old brick building on a busy city street; bowls full of fresh produce; groups of students who didn't look much older than me wearing kitchen whites and standing around counters full of food and utensils, listening intently to instructors. It looked incredible.

Now that I had the application, it was finally time to talk to my parents about culinary school. I knew Denise was right. I had to prove to them that this was the right decision for me. When I told Mom the next morning that I wanted to prepare a special meal for the family, she got all excited and offered to pay for the groceries. JP helped me plan a menu and a couple of nights later, on my night off, I got Mom and Alma to give me a hand in the kitchen.

"Have you enjoyed working for Denise?" Mom asked as I showed her how to peel garlic.

"Yeah, she's cool. She can get kind of grumpy when she's stressed, but she's still a great boss, and JP is awesome—he's taught me a lot."

"Well, it must be innate, because you sure didn't get that from your old mom."

"No kidding," said Alma. Mom flicked a garlic peel at her.

"I like cooking," I said. "I feel like I'm good at it."

"So tell me," Mom said, "are Denise and JP an item?"

I laughed. I'd wondered the same thing, but now that I knew Denise was gay, it was funny for me to even think about her as straight.

"What's so funny?"

"Nothing. It's just—I don't think Denise thinks about JP that way."

"You mean she's gay?"

I was surprised to hear her say it in such an offhand way.

"Yeah, I guess."

"Gay?" said Alma. "You mean as in homosexual? Like Elton John? In Deep Cove?"

"What's wrong with that?" I said.

"Nothing," said Alma. "It's just, I didn't think gay people lived in places like Deep Cove."

"Alma, honey," said Mom, "gay people live everywhere. They're just regular people like you and me."

Alma didn't say anything. She just stood there staring down at the carrots she was supposed to be peeling, thinking something through.

"Well, I can't say I'm surprised about Denise," my mom said. "A few of us suspected that was why she left town so quickly, back in the day. Good for her. It couldn't have been easy for her around here."

I didn't say anything, and I tried to act calm, but my heart was pounding against my rib cage. Did she know something? Did she suspect?

Thankfully, she saved me from having to respond. "How does this look?" she asked, showing me a pile of garlic that she'd minced.

"Looks good. Can you chop up a couple more cloves?" I glanced up and saw that Alma was now staring at me intently, chewing furiously on her lower lip. I quickly turned away and started rubbing the steaks with garlic and olive oil. It had never occurred to me that Alma might be the one to put it all together. I realized that I wasn't worried either way. Alma wasn't a bigmouth, and besides, there was no way she could know anything for sure.

Finally dinner was ready. My family sat patiently at the table while I served up mashed potatoes with goat cheese, roasted asparagus, and the steaks, pan-fried with a brandy peppercorn sauce. When I put the plates in front of them, they oohed and aahed. I waited as Dad poured the wine, including a splash for me, and we all toasted. When Dad cut into his steak, he said, "Man oh man, this looks like a great meal." He ate a few bites and then leaned back and looked at me. "That's probably one of the best steaks I've ever eaten."

I'd wanted to impress them, and from the way all three of them polished off their meals, I thought I had succeeded. When the main course was done, I brought out the *pièce de résistance*—a strawberry tart that JP had helped me make in the restaurant the day before.

After dinner, Mom made coffee and we sat around the table, relaxed and full.

"I've got to say," Dad said, leaning back in his chair again, "you've turned into quite the chef, Dan. Way to go."

"Thanks," I said. I took a deep breath. "What would you guys think if I wanted to do this for a living? I mean, be a chef. I really love it, and I think I'm good at it, and there's a really good school that I might be able to get into if I apply in the fall. JP says that there are lots of jobs, and you'll never be out of work if you're a chef and maybe someday I could be my own boss and have my own restaurant."

There was a long pause as my parents regarded each other across the table. I had no idea what they were thinking.

"What school?" my mom finally asked. I'd been waiting for this, and pulled the brochure from my backpack. I watched nervously as Mom looked over it and then passed it to Dad.

"Montreal?" Mom asked as Dad quietly flipped through the brochure.

"JP told me that they accept only twenty new students every year, and it's hard to get admitted straight from high school, but he thinks I can do it. He says I'm good enough, and if I fly up for the audition—"

"There's an audition?" my dad asked incredulously.

"Yeah, well, kind of. You have to go to the school and run through some exercises, and then they do an interview with you. They make you demonstrate techniques and stuff like that. JP told me I can stay with him if I get an interview. In Montreal."

"Okay, hang on. First of all, I haven't even met this JP guy, and now you're telling me you want to fly up to Montreal and stay with this—this cook, and apply to go to *cooking* school?"

I hadn't expected a quick approval. I'd figured I'd have to warm them up to it, but I hadn't expected this either. I could tell by his tone of voice that my dad didn't like the idea one bit. I was grateful when my mom cut in.

"Joe, hang on a minute. Let's at least find out a bit more about this. Danny, we're just a little bit surprised. This has never come up before."

"That's because I've never wanted to do anything this much before! I've never wanted to do *anything* before! But I'm good at it. I could be great at it."

"I'm not busting my ass in the middle of goddamned northern Alberta for eight months a year so you can cook filet mignon for rich assholes in some city in Quebec." Dad's face was flushed, and one of his hands was gripping the edge of the table.

"I thought you liked the filet mignon!"

"I did like it, it was great! Best steak I've ever eaten, and hopefully you'll cook us more of them someday.

But I'll be damned if you're going to take my money and spend it on some fruity-tootie school in Montreal!"

Alma snorted. "Fruity-tootie? Really?" she asked.

"Okay, what do *you* want me to do?" I asked.

"I want you to become a doctor or a lawyer or a teacher. Something that takes brains—something I wasn't smart enough to do!"

"Yeah, because it's all about you. Don't blame me because you lost your stupid job out west!"

"'Gentlemen,'" said Alma, "'you can't fight in here. This is the war room!'"

Mom glared at her and said, "Now is not the time, Alma."

My dad took a deep breath, and when he spoke again, he was obviously trying to control his anger. "Danny, do you think I like those jobs? Do you have any idea why I have to take those contracts in Alberta?"

"Because the bottling plant shut down."

"That's part of it, but the main thing is that I didn't have anything else to fall back on. I barely finished high school. But your mother and I have sacrificed a lot to raise you guys here."

"You didn't have to raise us here! This is what *you* guys wanted! Do you think I *like* it here in this shithole?"

I was standing now, and yelling. He didn't know the first thing about my life, but he was trying to tell me how to live. It was total bullshit.

"Trust me, Danny," he said, "you might think the rest of the world is a lot better than Deep Cove, but it's not. At least here you know where you come from."

"Yeah, it's pretty shocking that a work camp in northern Alberta doesn't live up to your standards. Thanks for the advice."

"Hey!" Mom said. "You are both completely over-reacting here!"

Dad didn't say anything for a moment. Then he stood up and looked down at all three of us. "You don't think I feel like a failure already?" he said quietly. "You don't think I wish I could go back and do everything all over again? I don't need you to tell me how unqualified I am to give you advice. Do what you want. I could care less."

He turned and walked out of the house, slamming the door behind him. After a moment, my mom got up and followed him.

"Good thing I didn't tell them I want to be an actress," said Alma, helping herself to another slice of strawberry tart.

NINETEEN

After the fight, Dad spent most of his waking hours in the garage, puttering around. When we were in the same room, we basically ignored each other.

"So much for family night," Alma said to me after a couple of awkward days. "It's like *Cat on a Hot Tin Roof* around here. Why don't you and Big Daddy just make up already?"

"I've got nothing to say to him," I told her.

"Suit yourself. For the record though, me and Big Mama think you're both actin' like a bunch of ornery houn' dogs."

I avoided home as much as possible. Since Lisa was constantly preoccupied with her mother, and Kierce was still out of town, Jay and I had begun hanging out pretty regularly with Maisie and Diana. They didn't have cool stories to tell about trips and concerts, but they were fun and easy to be around.

After the night at the lake, I'd worried that things would be awkward between me and Maisie, but it wasn't like that at all. "Just because you don't want to be my boyfriend doesn't mean we can't be friends, does it?" she asked me, laughing, when I brought it up.

Usually Jay ignored people when they gave him a hard time about smoking, but I noticed that when Maisie listed all the reasons he should quit, he actually seemed to pay attention. She also had some really good advice about how Jay could still finish high school with the rest of us. It turned out that Maisie was full of surprises.

Just when I was beginning to think I'd never spend any more time with Lisa, she invited me, out of the blue, to a party at her aunt's house.

"It's going to be really fun," she told me at work one afternoon. "My aunt is awesome, and she has lots of cool friends. Best of all, my brother's going to be there. He flew in for a few days. I totally want you to meet him; I've told him all about you."

Lisa's aunt lived on a stretch of coastal road a few miles outside of Deep Cove. My mom dropped me off at the bottom of a long gravel driveway that was packed with cars. I walked up the hill toward a large wooden house and past a verandah filled with small groups of laughing people.

I found Lisa in the backyard underneath a huge oak tree hung with white lights, talking to a bunch of people my parents' age. She excused herself from the group and came over to greet me.

"Thank god you're here. If I had to answer one more question about my 'plans for the future,' I would have killed someone. Here, come meet my aunt." I followed her across the lawn to a tall, graceful-looking woman with an unruly mass of curly gray hair. She was wearing a flowing dress covered with bright multicolored flowers and holding a gigantic wineglass.

"Now who have we here?" she asked.

Lisa introduced me, and we made small talk for a minute before her aunt moved on to greet some new guests. "Lisa," she said, "please find your mother and tell her to stop hiding inside."

"Come on," Lisa told me, "I'll find my mom and then we'll head down to the beach." I followed her as she worked her way through the crowd toward the house. The back door led into a warm, well-used kitchen. Open shelves lined the walls, stacked high with bright pottery dishes and dozens of wineglasses in all shapes and sizes. Against one wall was a large, rustic-looking wooden table with mismatched chairs pulled up around it, and above it hung a massive abstract painting, the paint brushed and scraped on it so thick that it seemed to jump off the canvas. This was the kind of house I wanted to live in someday.

Lisa led me down a narrow hallway into a dimly lit living room, where scratchy old jazz floated out the open windows. I didn't notice the woman hidden in the shadows until Lisa spoke to her.

"There you are, Mom. Aunt Cheryl is asking for you."

Lisa's mother was very slight, smaller than either her daughter or her sister, and her face looked tired. She was holding a glass of some sort of dark-brown booze.

"I'm sure she is. Christ, that woman has too much energy." She laughed grimly and glanced over at me.

"You two are so lucky," she said to me. "It's such a blessing to be young, with your whole lives ahead of you." She stood up and walked over to us, reaching up to brush her hand through Lisa's hair. "Take advantage of it while you can." She gave me a tired but sincere smile.

"That's great, Mom. I always enjoy your life lessons. Now why don't you go out and get yourself some food? People are wondering where the guest of honor is hiding."

Her mother sighed, "I will." She turned back to me, her voice noticeably softer. "I'm sorry. It's been a rough year. Lisa, give me one of those cigarettes, will you?" I watched, amazed, as Lisa rummaged in her bag and produced her pack of French cigarettes. My mother would have locked me in the cellar if she'd ever caught me smoking.

"Jesus H. Christ," said Lisa as she led me toward the front door and down the steps of the verandah. "I'd have introduced you to her, but she wouldn't remember your name."

Lisa had described her mom as unhinged and bitchy, but to me she just seemed a bit sad but totally pleasant. It made me think about my dad. Was it possible that he wasn't as bad as I thought he was? Was my impression of him as out of whack as Lisa's was of her mom? Or was the truth somewhere in the middle?

I followed Lisa across the lawn in front of the house. It sloped down toward the water and became a field thick with goldenrod, Queen Anne's lace and massive tangles of wild roses. Lisa stopped, reached down into a clump of grass and pulled out a couple of bottles of wine.

"I stole them this afternoon when the party preparations were in full swing."

She led the way through the field and down a path to the rocky beach, where a whole different party seemed to be happening. A couple of girls were jumping around in the water, and a few other people sat around a pile of driftwood that looked as if it had been prepared for a bonfire. Someone was strumming a guitar, and a bottle of wine was being passed around.

We walked up to the group by the bonfire, and my heart skipped a beat as a tall shirtless guy walked across the beach to us. He was possibly the hottest guy I'd ever seen, tanned and muscular with shaggy red hair, a big toothy smile, and Lisa's perfect green eyes.

"So this must be the famous Danny?" He extended his hand, and we shook. "I'm Will, Lisa's brother."

He was holding a joint. He puffed on it, then held it out to us. Lisa took a hit and then passed it to me. I hesitated for a moment, then reached out and pinched it between my thumb and index finger, the way they'd done. I'd never smoked pot before, but there was no way I was going to look like a narc in front of Lisa's hot brother. I took a drag and coughed, but managed to pull myself together. I passed it back to Will and felt a charge run down my spine when his fingers grazed against mine.

Lisa dragged me over to introduce me to the rest of the group. Everyone was really friendly, but it was clear from the way they talked that they came from a different world than I did. They spoke about the Ivy League universities they went to and the trips they'd recently taken and the Broadway shows they'd been to. Deep Cove was obviously just a quick side trip in their sparkly lives.

More joints were passed around, along with wine and a bottle of sweet dark rum. Before long, I was pretty messed up. Luckily it was getting dark, and I was able to sit quietly with my back up against a big piece of driftwood.

Lisa was laughing with a couple of girls on the other side of the circle. My eyes drifted toward her brother where he stood around the fire with some of the other guys.

He turned and saw me looking and came over to sit down next to me.

"Man, what a night, hey?" he said.

"You can say that again."

"So Lisa tells me you're an up-and-coming chef."

I laughed. "Not exactly. She's got an active imagination."

"Yeah, well she's got a way of making things sound great, that's for sure."

I didn't know what he meant. Had Lisa talked to him about me? Had she made me sound like a guy she could be interested in? I didn't care. I was more interested in him after five minutes than I'd ever be in his sister.

"So have you met our mom?" Will asked.

"Yeah, just tonight, up in the house."

"She's a piece of work. She and Lisa don't get along most of the time, but they're more alike than either of them would ever admit."

It was none of my business, so all I said was, "How long are you staying?"

"Couple of days. Hopefully I'll get to see a bit of Lisa before I leave. She's a pretty popular girl."

What was he talking about? Lisa had told me she'd been spending all of her free time at Cheryl's house. If that wasn't true, where *had* she been?

"So you grew up around here, huh?" asked Will.

"Yeah, pretty much. Born and raised."

"Lucky guy."

I figured he was joking, but when I looked at him, his expression was sincere.

"That's something coming from somebody who grew up in, like, the coolest city on the planet," I said.

"Well, I guess the grass is always greener on the other side, right? Big city like that, there's not much time to stop and think. Sometimes it's hard to figure out what's really going on in your head, what you should be doing with your life."

"Hey, I don't have a clue, and I've got lots of time to think about it."

"Well, shit," he said, "there goes my plan to move to Deep Cove and figure out the secret of life." We both laughed.

Lisa came over and plunked down between us. "Will, are you flirting with my friend?" I blushed at the question, but he laughed at her.

"Lisa, you think I'm flirting with your friends every time I talk to them."

"Well, don't go corrupting my little Danny here."

Will jumped to his feet. "If you'll excuse me, I have some work to do." My heart sank as I watched him walk over to the fire and start flirting with Shyla, a beautiful dark-skinned girl in an embroidered dress.

"Will's been totally hitting on Shyla since he got here," said Lisa. "They're totally going to do it."

"She's pretty hot," I said.

"Yeah, she's okay. Kind of full of herself, but whatever. So are you having fun?" Lisa asked me.

"Yeah, for sure," I said. "Everyone's really cool. I love your aunt's house. Thanks for inviting me."

"It wouldn't be the same without you," she said.

"Any idea when Kierce is going to be home?" I asked her.

"No. He's left me a couple of messages," she said vaguely, "but I haven't called him back." She stood up.

"Come on, let's go up to the house and get something to eat. I'm starving."

As we walked back up the hill, I glanced back at the group on the beach. I wasn't one of those people yet, but I knew that I wanted to be. I hoped I wouldn't have to wait too long.

TWENTY

In the car while driving me to work the morning after the party, my mom handed me an envelope.

"What's this?" I asked.

"It's your application fee. To cooking school."

I opened it up. Sure enough, it was a check for fifty dollars, made out to the Atwater Culinary Institute.

"For the record," Alma said from the backseat, "I contributed five bucks toward that."

"And I swiped a symbolic twenty from your dad's wallet," said Mom. "All three of us are helping you with this, whether we're all fully aware of it or not."

"I don't understand," I said.

"Come on, Danny," she said, "do you think I'm going to

miss out on the chance to have a classically trained chef in the family? The only requirement is that *you* have to cook the Christmas turkey every year for the rest of our lives."

"That was my idea," said Alma. "No more repeats of the '92 holiday disaster. Or as I like to call it, 'The Towering Inferno.'"

"What about Dad?" I asked.

"What about him?" said Mom. "He's not the only member of this family. More importantly, he only contributed fifty percent of your DNA, and a total of zero percent of the pregnancy and lengthy delivery required to pop you out into the world."

"Okay, gross," said Alma.

"The point," my mom went on, "is that I'd like to think that I have some input into your future. As far as I'm concerned, you becoming a chef is a great idea. Even if your dad is absolutely right and cooking school turns out to be a terrible idea, you have your whole life to come up with a Plan B."

"I'm sorry," I said, "I just never thought that you were that interested in what I did for a living."

"Are you kidding me? There are few things more interesting to me than what my two fabulous children make of themselves."

"'A boy's best friend is his mother,' Danny," said Alma.

"Did it ever occur to you," said Mom, "that I'm just not that worried about you?"

"Well, Dad sure is."

"You have to understand, Danny. Your dad loves you. He wants nothing more than for you to have a wonderful, happy, fulfilling life. The problem is, he overthinks everything. Sometimes you two are so alike that it makes the back of my head quiver."

"What?" I said. "Are you kidding me? Dad and I have nothing in common!"

Mom and Alma both snorted at the same time. "As if," said Alma.

"Just because you don't have the same hobbies or interests," said Mom, "doesn't mean you aren't practically the same person sometimes. First of all, you've both been sulking like children since your big blowup. Then there's the fact that the two of you worry about absolutely everything. You could both stand to have a little faith that things will work themselves out."

"Don't forget the earlobe thing," said Alma.

Mom laughed. "She's right. When you guys are concentrating on something, you both twist your earlobes the same way. It's pretty funny."

Dad did that. *I* didn't do that. Did I?

She pulled into the Sandbar parking lot. "Listen,

Danny, cut your dad some slack. He's been pretty down on himself lately. I keep telling him not to worry, things are going to be fine, but he hates the uncertainty right now. We'll pull through, we always do. And so," she said, reaching over to twist my ear, "will you."

I got out of the car with my head spinning. Did my dad and I *really* have that much in common?

I heard Ken laughing through the open window as I approached the restaurant.

"Maybe we'll go back to—what did you call it?—the Spot," he was saying. "*That* was pretty impressive."

At the mention of the Spot, I stopped and stood outside the window to listen.

"No way," I heard Lisa say. "That was stupid."

"I don't understand why we have to keep sneaking around," said Ken. "It's so high school."

"It's just easier than getting people all upset."

I walked in, and they both turned at the sound of the door. Lisa's face turned red when she saw me, and she pushed past Ken through the swinging door into the kitchen.

"Hey, Danny," said Ken. I ignored him and followed Lisa. She'd grabbed a cloth and was busy pretending to polish silverware.

"What was that all about?" I asked.

"What do you mean?" she said.

"Did you take Ken to the Spot?" I asked. Everything made sense all of a sudden: Lisa lying about spending all that time with her mother; the condom wrapper Jay had found.

She sighed and put her cloth down. "It just kind of happened. I really like him, and we're having some fun, that's all."

"Doesn't Ken have a girlfriend? Don't *you* have a boyfriend?"

"You mean Kierce? Oh god, give me a break. I told you, I'll talk to him as soon as he gets back to town. And things with Ken and his girlfriend have been going downhill for months."

That was news to me. Ken was always talking about how hot his girlfriend was, and how he couldn't wait to see her again when he went back to university in the fall.

"I can't believe you took him to the Spot," I said.

"What difference does it make? It was just a place to go. You don't own it, you know." She walked over and ruffled my hair. "Danny, come on, please don't be childish. I wanted to tell you, but I was waiting for a good opportunity. That's why I invited you to the party at Cheryl's house, but we were having so much fun, it didn't seem like the right time. I really care about you, but this is none of your business."

She pulled me into a hug.

"Please don't ruin everything by being mad at me."

"WOW," SAID MAISIE that night when I told her and Jay what was going on. "That's pretty low."

"Yeah," I said. "I don't know what to do. Should we try to get in touch with Kierce?"

"Just let Lisa handle it," said Jay. "It's their business. Kierce isn't stupid; he knew something was up before he left for Ontario. I don't think he'll really care that much. He's been away for a week, and summer's almost over. What does he think is going to happen?"

Jay was right, but I didn't feel good about keeping it to myself, especially after Kierce had asked me to keep him in the loop. As it turned out, I didn't have much time to think about it.

The next night after work, Maisie helped me clean up the kitchen so we could get out of there quickly. Diana and Jay were picking us up after our shift ended.

"See you guys tomorrow," said Lisa, stopping into the kitchen to grab her coat.

"Hey, Lisa," said Maisie. "You should come out with us after work sometime. We miss you!"

"Soon, I promise," said Lisa, walking over to where we were polishing wineglasses. "I'm terrible. I've been kind of preoccupied." She looked at me and smiled.

Maisie and I finished up and walked out of the restaurant about ten minutes later.

"Oh shit," said Maisie. I turned and saw Kierce's van parked next to Lisa's car. Diana's car pulled into the parking lot, and she and Jay got out just as Kierce jumped out of Lisa's car. He had a bunch of flowers in one hand, and he hurled them onto the ground. Lisa got out of her car and stood awkwardly next to it.

"Get away from me!" he yelled.

She started to walk toward him, but he held his hand up, palm out, to stop her.

"Go!"

She hesitated, then got into her car and pulled out of the parking lot.

Jay and I walked over to him. He was pacing in a circle, and as we approached, he stopped and looked at us. I was surprised to see that his eyes were glistening.

"Come on, man, calm down," said Jay.

"Don't fucking tell me to calm down! What do you know about it anyway?"

Neither of us said anything. He stopped in his tracks, turned and looked right at us.

"Did you guys know about this?"

"We didn't find out until after you were gone, Kierce," I told him.

He looked at me with disbelief.

"You mean you guys knew about this, and neither of you bothered to tell me?"

"Kierce, come on, we figured it was her job to tell you."

"So my two best friends didn't think I deserved to know she was screwing around on me?"

"It wasn't like that at all," Jay said. In the background, Maisie and Diana stood watching us.

"Do you know what?" he asked, walking up to me and poking his finger at my chest. "I thought you had my back. I really believed that. Joke's on me, right?"

"Kierce, come on," I said. "You aren't making any sense."

"Unbelievable. Rule Ten: Who needs enemies with friends like you guys?"

He walked over to his van and got in, spinning his tires as he took off out of the parking lot.

"What the hell just happened?" asked Jay.

I TRIED CALLING KIERCE the next day, and the day after that, but his mom kept making excuses, and he didn't return my calls or Jay's.

Driving across town with the girls, we would sometimes see him cruising around with Ferris and some of
their hockey buddies, laughing and drinking beer.
Occasionally he'd glance at Maisie's car and then turn
away without acknowledging us.

"He's being a total dickhead," said Lisa when I told her
what was going on. She obviously didn't care whether she
ever saw Kierce again or not.

"Well, he's still my friend," I said, "and I feel bad
for him."

"Bad because he decided to blame you for something
that wasn't your fault? Danny, things don't always end up
all neat and tidy. He probably wasn't much of a friend to
begin with, if he's treating you like this." She headed back
out to the dining room with an order of desserts.

Jay saw it differently. "Who cares, man? Kierce will
come around. He's just pissed off about Lisa. By the time
school rolls around again and she's back in New York,
it will be like it never happened."

Something told me it wouldn't be that simple.

TWENTY-ONE

"Are you guys heading down to the beach party?" Lisa asked me as Maisie and I prepared to leave work.

It was the last Saturday of August, and there was going to be a big end-of-summer party at the beach, one last blowout before school started up again after Labor Day.

"You bet," said Maisie. "It's going to be super fun!"

"Why don't you come with us?" I asked Lisa. "It'll be packed. Jay and Diana are already there. You could bring Ken."

"You're sweet," she said, "but it's his last shift, so we're going to go hang out together somewhere." She flashed me a genuine smile, and I felt a pang of sadness that things had ended up this way.

"You never know," she said, "maybe we'll show up later on." I doubted it. Ken obviously thought he was way too cool to hang out with us.

"I don't understand what Lisa sees in Ken anyway," Maisie told me as we crossed the road and headed through the sand dunes toward the far end of the beach. "He's such a jerk!"

"Yeah, no kidding."

"She and Kierce were weird too, I never understood them being together. Maybe she just likes to test out different kinds of guys."

"Who knows?" I said. I'd given up trying to understand what Lisa was looking for.

"So you're still not talking to him?" Maisie asked.

"Kierce? It's more like he's not talking to me."

"All because of the Lisa thing? That's so stupid. There must be something more to it than that."

"Like what?"

"Who knows, but it's obviously not your fault that Lisa was screwing around with Ken. I don't know why he's punishing you."

I wondered if she was right. If something else *was* bothering Kierce, I couldn't for the life of me figure out what it would be.

184

"Hey," said Maisie, "do you want to go up into the sand dunes and have a drink before we head down to the party?"

We scrambled up into the dunes and set ourselves up in a hollow surrounded by sea grass. From where we sat, we could see down the beach toward the already growing bonfire. Thick clusters of clouds drifted lazily across the moon, and the tide kept up a steady rushing pulse. Sitting there with the sea air wafting up into my nose, I wondered how I would ever leave this place. For a few moments, it was hard to imagine anywhere more perfect on Earth.

Maisie had arranged for her cousin to buy some booze for us, and I was pretty happy when she opened up her backpack and pulled out a big bottle of Raspberry Comet Cooler. She cracked it and took a swig, then passed it to me.

"Sorry, I'm sure you'd rather have beer."

"I don't mind. This is fine. I actually prefer this stuff."

We passed it back and forth between us for a while, not saying much. Off in the distance, the bonfire had grown. We were well hidden in our perch, but we could see people making their way along the beach toward the fire, unaware that we were only a few feet away from them. The light from the bonfire flickered at us through the darkness. The wind picked up, and it started to get colder.

After a while, I asked her, "Do you think we should go down to the party?"

"Let's just stay a few minutes longer." She lay down on the sand and I followed, lying down next to her, watching as the sky filled up with clouds. Maisie wiggled closer to me. "I'm chilly!" she said. Before I knew it, she'd rolled sideways and we were kissing. She tasted sweet, like the liquor, and for a few minutes, we rolled around, tangled and laughing and grabbing at each other. Then I pulled back.

"What's the matter?"

"I don't know, Maisie. I don't think this is a good idea."

She sat up, propping herself on her elbows. "It's Lisa, isn't it?"

"No."

"Hey, it's okay! I'm not going to be offended. I think it's kind of sweet if you like someone so much that you don't want to fool around with anyone else. It's like, loyal, or something."

"That's not it."

She just looked at me, and there was something about her face—kind and sweet and trustworthy—that made me feel safe.

"I think I might be gay," I blurted out.

"Really? Wow!"

I nodded, and maybe it was because I was kind of drunk, or maybe it was because everything with Kierce and Lisa and my dad caught up with me, or maybe it was because I'd never said the words aloud to anyone before, but I started to cry. Maisie leaned over and gave me a big hug.

"Oh my god. Hey, don't cry. It's okay!"

"I guess I've always known," I told her, wiping my face with the back of my hand. "Or at least since I was twelve or thirteen. But I managed to convince myself it wasn't true. Couldn't be true. It's hard to explain."

"It's okay, you don't have to explain."

It felt so good to talk to somebody about it, to say all the things that had been bottled up in my brain for years. Maisie understood what it was like to grow up in Deep Cove, how difficult it was for someone to be different.

Something else crossed my mind. "Maisie…"

"Hey, don't even say it. I'm not going to say a word to anyone. Not even to the girls." She laughed. "Especially the girls." She looked me in the eye. "I promise you. I promise. I know how that would go over around here. I wouldn't do that to you."

I knew that I could trust her, and I also felt kind of bad that I'd misjudged her. That I'd listened to Lisa badmouth her.

"Let's head to the party," I said.

"Are you sure? If you'd rather just go somewhere and talk, I would totally do that."

"Thanks, but I think we should go. I feel really good; I feel like we should go somewhere and celebrate."

"First time I've ever celebrated being turned down by a guy!" She stood and grabbed my hands to pull me up. We brushed the sand off our backs and headed down through the dunes to the beach.

The party was in full swing when we got there. A couple of people had brought guitars, and a sing-along was happening by the fire, a massive flaming pile of driftwood. Even from several feet away, it held back some of the chill in the air.

I saw Jay and walked over to him.

"I was wondering if you were going to make it," he said.

"Yeah, Maisie and I were up in the dunes, having a drink," I told him. He raised an eyebrow. "Nothing happened," I said, laughing. "Seriously, she and I are just friends."

I glanced across the fire and saw Lisa walking toward us.

"What are you doing here?" I asked. "I thought you had plans with Ken."

"Yeah, well, he had different plans. Whatever."

"Did you guys split up?"

"I guess you could say that. Serves me right. I don't know what I expected to happen. Anyway, life goes on, right?"

It was actually kind of great to just relax with everyone, Lisa included. My talk with Maisie had taken some weight off my shoulders, and even though I hadn't spent much time with Lisa lately, having her there seemed like the right way to end the summer. The only thing missing was Kierce. I tried to put him out of my head.

Then he showed up, staggering into the middle of the party with Ferris and some of their buddies. He was drinking straight from a bottle of Captain Morgan and laughing loudly. People stopped and looked over at him. He was obviously really messed up. He pushed through the crowd and walked over to where we were standing.

"Oh, will you look who it is? My excellent friends!" he said. "I might as well tell you all the big news. I'm moving to Ontario. Good riddance, right?"

"Whoa, what do you mean?" asked Jay.

"That's what the big trip to see my grandparents was all about," he said. "My mom is leaving the old man, so we're getting the fuck out of Dodge."

He looked at Lisa as if he had only just noticed her. "Oh hey, Lisa! Where's your new boyfriend, you whore?"

"Fuck you, Kierce," she said.

"Why don't you go sleep it off, Kierce?" I asked him.

He laughed. "Are you kidding me? Are you going to defend her?" He looked at her. "If you're planning on doing *him* next, you should know that it's a lost cause. My man here is a total faggot."

And that was it. I lunged at him, screaming and punching wildly. He was taken by surprise, and we both fell backward. We rolled around on the ground, throwing punches and jockeying for space. I vaguely heard the girls screaming at us to stop, and then I felt someone—maybe Jay—reach in and try to pull me out. I threw him back, and after a few failed attempts to break us up, everybody just stood back and let us have at it.

I'd never been in a fight before, but I didn't care, I was beyond thinking. Everything moved in slow motion, and it was almost as if I wasn't even in the middle of it, but watching from the sidelines. Kierce managed to get to his feet, and when I stood up, he connected with my face and I was knocked backward. From the ground, I jumped for his legs, and he lost his footing. Somehow I managed to get on top of him, my knees pressing on his chest, my arms holding him down at the elbows. He squirmed to move, and when he shifted sideways, I hauled back and punched him in the side of the head.

Somehow, I was dragged away, kicking out at the air, my arms held behind my back. For a few minutes I struggled, and when it was clear that I'd calmed down and the fight was over, I was let go. I dropped to my knees, my chest heaving. I put my hand up to my face and realized that it was wet. I could taste blood, mixed with salt. I could tell that tears were running down my cheeks, but I wasn't really crying.

My ribs were burning, and I puked, retching and spitting into the sand. Someone bent down beside me and put a hand on my back, and I was aware for the first time of people standing around looking at me.

"Are you okay?" Maisie asked quietly.

"Leave me alone," I managed to sputter, standing up and starting to walk down the beach.

I didn't make it far before Lisa was beside me. "Come on," she said, lifting my arm over her neck and helping me as I hobbled along. I looked sideways at her, and was struck by how she no longer looked like someone who'd dropped into Deep Cove from another world; she just looked like any other girl at our school. She looked like the rest of us.

I let her help me along for a few feet. Then I pulled away. "This is your fault!" I said. "Why did you come here? Do you even care what you did? Go back where you came from!"

She let go of me and stepped back.

"Jesus, Danny, will you *please* just shut the fuck up!" she said.

I stopped in my tracks, not knowing what to say.

"Listen to yourself!" she went on. "Do you really think this is my fault? You think this happened because I screwed around on Kierce? Okay, fine, so I'm a bitch and Kierce is mad at me, gotcha. It wasn't very nice of me. But what the hell do you think that has to do with you?" She walked over to me and put her hand on my shoulder. "Instead of feeling sorry for yourself and blaming people for shit, why don't you try showing yourself some respect, so you can move the fuck on with your life?"

I stared at her, stunned.

"I'm sorry," I managed to stammer.

"See, that's what I'm talking about. Nobody needs to be sorry for anything."

She turned and walked away along the beach toward the parking lot. I stood watching her as she moved away down the beach. Then Maisie ran up and grabbed me by the shoulder.

"Diana has her car. She and Jay are going to come and get you. Stay here, we'll be right back."

She went running back along the beach, and I dropped down and sat on the ground. After a few minutes, Jay was kneeling down next to me.

"You okay, buddy? Come on, you can crash at my house tonight."

I nodded. He helped me up, and they walked with me to Diana's car. As Diana pulled out of the parking lot, the sky opened up and it began to pour.

TWENTY-TWO

I woke up on the couch at Jay's house the next morning with a fat lip and a throbbing cheek. I figured I looked like hell, but when I looked in the mirror, it didn't bother me as much as I expected. There was a cut in my lip, and the hint of a bluish-green bruise spread from my eye down my cheek. I could tell it would look a lot worse in a day or two. I looked tough. It wasn't even close to the truth, but I liked the illusion.

Jay's dad drove me home. When I walked around to the back of the house, Alma and my parents were on the deck eating breakfast. My mom took one look at my face and gasped.

"Oh my god, Danny, what happened?" she asked, jumping out of her chair.

"I don't want to talk about it," I said.

I looked warily at my dad, expecting some kind of lecture, but instead he just stared at me as if he couldn't believe what he was seeing.

"Who'd'a thunkit?" said Alma. "'You coulda been a contenda!'"

"This isn't funny," said Mom. "Danny, I don't even know what to say about this!"

"You don't have to say anything," I said. "It's my business, and it's over, and that's all there is to it. Now I have to take a nap."

But I couldn't sleep. Every time I closed my eyes, I felt a faint rush of adrenaline as I visualized hitting Kierce and being punched back. In the middle of all of last night's excitement, I'd almost forgotten about coming out to Maisie. So much had happened, I didn't know what to think about anything anymore.

There was a knock on the door to my room, and my dad stuck his head in.

"Can I come in?"

"Yeah."

He grabbed my desk chair and pulled it over by

my bed. "I'd hate to see the other guy," he said with a slight smile.

I laughed. "I doubt he looks worse than me. Mom's pretty pissed off, hey?"

"Oh, she'll be fine," he said. "I just reminded her about the time back in high school when I beat the crap out of some guy who was making eyes at her. It was probably a pretty stupid thing to do, but she didn't seem to mind it back then."

"I guess they're right about you and me having more in common than we think," I said.

He laughed. "I guess so."

We didn't say anything for a minute.

"Danny, I'm not going to lie to you," he said, finally. "I don't like this cooking school thing one bit."

I groaned and turned toward the wall.

"Hang on!" he said. "Hear me out."

I flipped back over and looked at him warily.

"I still think," he went on, "that university is the way to go, especially if you want to have a good solid foundation and lots of opportunities."

"Yeah, Dad, I know. You've said that a million times."

He held out his hand to shut me up. "Just let me finish. Anyway, I looked through that brochure you gave us, and as far as I can tell, it seems like, if you *have* to go to cooking school, this Atwater place is the one to go to. Am I right?"

"Yeah. JP says it's the best one in the country."

"It looks like it might be tough to get in. Think you can do it?"

"I'm not sure," I said. "But I think I'd have a pretty good shot. JP's been teaching me a lot. I'd like to try."

"Well, like I said, I'm not thrilled about the idea, but your mother and I had a talk, and she made the very reasonable point that if this cooking thing doesn't pan out, you can always go back to university later on."

"That's true," I said. I knew that wouldn't happen, but I figured if it made him feel good, it didn't hurt to let him think it.

"I just have one condition," he said. "I want you to apply to a couple of universities too. Just to keep your options open. Sound like a deal?"

I didn't need to think about it. I reached over and gave him a firm handshake.

"Deal," I said.

"Atta boy."

THE TOURIST SEASON was over, and JP was preparing to go back to Montreal. Denise was going to stick around

Deep Cove for the winter, but planned to close the Sandbar down until the following summer.

After our last shift, Lisa, Maisie, Denise and I sat around in the kitchen as JP prepared one last meal for us.

"I don't know what I'm going to do without you next year, JP," said Denise.

"What do you mean?" he said. "I'm open to offers. I just have three conditions. Number one, you give me a raise. Number two, Danny comes back to be my sous chef again. If he's going to go to cooking school, there's a lot more I need to teach him first. Number three, you fill up my wineglass, pronto."

We all laughed, and Denise reached for the bottle.

"I totally want to come back and work for you next year, Denise," said Maisie. "This has been the best summer job ever!"

"Me too," I said. "I wouldn't miss it."

"I can't tell you how awesome that is, guys," said Denise.

"What about you, Lisa?" asked Maisie. "Are you going to come back and spend next summer in Deep Cove?"

Lisa looked a little bit sad. "Probably not," she said. "My aunt is selling her place so that she can move back to New York and be closer to my mom. That's great and all, but I doubt I'll be back. It's okay though," she said, her face brightening. "My friend Naomi and I are planning on backpacking around India next summer."

"I want to make a toast!" said JP. "To a group of wonderful young people, and their beautiful futures." His eyes started to fill with tears.

"Oh boy, here we go," said Denise. "The old French bastard has had too much wine again."

"Be quiet, you evil woman," he said, standing up and holding out his glass. "To good food, good friends and the promise of youth. What more does one need in life?"

"Cheers!" we all yelled, clinking glasses.

After supper, Lisa offered me a ride. "Last one of the summer," she said.

As I was grabbing my coat, JP asked me to come back into the kitchen with him. "I have a little something for you," he said. One at a time, he picked up the knives that I'd been using all summer, and wrapped them up in their old stained cloth.

"These are for you," he said, passing the bundle to me. "Use them until you can afford a newer set. I can't wait to taste what you do with them. You've been a great sous chef, my friend. I'm very proud of you." He patted me on the back.

I looked down at the knives and felt my eyes start to itch. When he'd first given them to me, weeks earlier, they'd seemed like a crappy secondhand set. Now that I'd learned so much with them, I could understand what they must have meant to JP. He'd obviously carried them around with him for years for a reason, and now he was passing them on to me. It was hard to believe that anyone could have that much faith in me. I hoped I could live up to it.

Before taking me home, Lisa drove down to our usual place at the beach so she could have her nightly cigarette.

"It's been a pretty crazy summer," she said.

"You can say that again."

"So I was thinking. You should come stay with me in New York for a week sometime this year."

"Sounds great."

"I'm serious, Danny. Come visit me. I'll show you the city! You can meet my friends!"

I didn't answer, and she let it drop. We both knew it wouldn't happen.

Neither of us said anything for a while. I wondered if I would ever see Lisa again. Or even think about her in ten years. Or Kierce. Even Jay, for that matter. Deep Cove was now. Who knew what would happen next?

As if she could read my mind, Lisa said, "You know what? In a month or two, you might not remember me. None of you."

Maybe she was right. Maybe it didn't matter either way.

"Oh, hey!" she said, "Speaking of that, I almost forgot, I have something for you!" she grabbed her bag from the backseat and dug around for a second, then pulled something out, hiding it from me behind her back.

"I made this for you because I don't *want* you to forget me." She thrust something at me.

It was a mix tape like the ones she and her friends exchanged, but this one had been made specifically for me. I opened it up and unfolded the paper cover inside the case. I could tell she'd spent a lot of time making it. An elaborate patchwork of images included a magazine cutout of the I Heart NYC logo next to a small paper map of Cape Breton Island. She'd cut the Sandbar sign out of a photograph of the restaurant, and it was glued next to a picture of a Model T Ford with "Old Bessie" written overtop in curlicued letters. In the middle of it all, carefully written in big block letters intertwined with tiny little vines and flowers, it said, *For Danny, With Love, From His New Best Friend—XOXOXO Lisa—Summer '94*

"Wow." It was only a mix tape, but it felt like the best gift anyone had ever given me.

"Look!" She grabbed the paper and flipped it over. On the reverse, she'd written down all the songs and musicians, and she'd named each side. Side A was *Learn to Dance*, and Side B was *Learn to Cook*.

"Some of these are songs that we've already listened to, but most of them I don't think you know yet. So the first side is songs that are good for dancing, obviously, and the other side is full of songs from JP's collection. He helped me pick some of them out!"

"I don't know what to say. Thank you. Seriously."

She clapped her hands again. "I'm so happy you like it! Let's put it on!"

She grabbed the tape and shoved it into the stereo, and the air filled up with horns and drums.

Baby, everything is all right, uptight, out of sight.

"Stevie!" I yelled.

She smiled and nodded. "You got it!"

She jumped out of the car and ran around to my side. "Come on!" she yelled, pulling me out of the car.

And then, under the late summer sky, we danced as if neither of us had a care in the world.

TWENTY-THREE

"Things are going to change. Big-time. Just wait and see. By the end of this year, you won't even recognize me."

"What makes you say that?" I asked.

"Danny, everyone knows that ninth grade is when a girl blossoms into a young lady, full of spirit and vitality."

It was Labor Day, the last day of summer vacation. In anticipation of her first year in high school, Alma had been driving us all crazy by incessantly humming "To Sir, With Love," for almost a week. I didn't have the heart to tell her that Mr. Blanchette, her new home-room teacher, was less like Sidney Poitier and more like Joe Pesci.

I watched as she carefully stirred milk into a bowl of crumbled flour and butter. "You know," she said, "this is going to be a big year for you too, big brother. One last year of tying up loose ends before hitting the big wide world, just like Jimmy Stewart in *It's a Wonderful Life*."

"Careful," I said, "don't overmix it." I helped her dump the dough onto the floured counter, and showed her how to knead it lightly with the palms of her hands.

"I thought the whole thing about *It's a Wonderful Life* is that he never manages to get out of the town," I said.

"Yeah, well, I'm still kind of hoping that you decide to stick around."

"Wow, Alma, I'm touched."

"It's mainly selfish," she said. "I'm not sure if I can survive three years of Mom's food. Why do you think I asked you to teach me how to cook?"

We cut the dough into rounds and popped the biscuits into the oven. The phone rang, and I brushed off my hands on my apron and answered it. It was Jay.

"Kierce asked me to call you," he said. "He wants us to meet him at the Spot."

"Are you kidding me? I thought I'd be the last person he'd want to see."

"Yeah, me too, but he's leaving tomorrow."

"I don't know," I said. I was still feeling a bit sore from the fight. "I'm not sure it's a good idea. Maybe he'll try to kick my ass or something."

"Give me a break. Come on, Dan. He's leaving for good. It'll be fine. Clear the air a little bit."

I didn't know if I even cared if the air was clear, but I agreed to go with him.

Kierce was sitting under the bridge when we got there. I was secretly pleased to see that he had a major shiner and a fat lip. He laughed when he saw me.

"Man, I guess it was a pretty fair fight, hey, Dan?"

"Yeah, I guess." I still felt a little bit weird about being there.

"Relax, man," he said. "It was just a fight."

"Am I going to have to break you guys up again?" said Jay.

"No, it's cool," I said. "We're cool."

"That's my man!" said Kierce, reaching out and giving me a slap on the back.

"So you're really leaving, hey?" asked Jay.

"Yep. Looks that way," said Kierce. "Tomorrow morning. What a pain in the ass." He sighed and leaned back against the wall.

"Why didn't you tell us?" I asked.

"Shit, I don't know. Everything went to hell when I freaked out at you guys outside the restaurant," he said. "I was so pissed off at my parents, and then I thought I'd at least be able to hang out with you guys for my last few weeks. I guess I screwed that up pretty bad."

"It wasn't like we were trying to keep anything a secret, Kierce," I said. "I tried to get Lisa to tell you."

"Yeah, I know. I was just being stupid. She was pretty clear the whole thing with me and her didn't mean anything to her. I was just too stubborn to believe it. Anyway, I'm sorry I blamed you guys. It was totally stupid of me. I guess I just felt like the whole world was against me."

"S'okay," I said.

"The worst part is, I really did like her, a lot," he said. "I never felt that way about a girl before. I probably overdid it with the love talk, but I was into her big-time."

He looked genuinely sad, and I found myself feeling really bad for the guy. Kierce might have talked a big game, but when you got down to it, he had his own hang-ups just like the rest of us.

"So what happens now?" asked Jay.

"We're going to live with my jerk-ass grandparents for a while until my mom can find us a place of our own."

"That sucks," I said. I meant it. I didn't know what I'd do if I had to finish high school somewhere other than Deep Cove.

"It'll be okay," he said. "The high school looks pretty cool. They have a football team, and there's a lot more shit to do there. Malls, movie theaters, paintball. We'll be pretty close to Toronto too. Think of all the girls! You guys will totally have to come visit me!"

"Sounds good, man," said Jay. I nodded. I figured I was as likely to visit Kierce in Ontario as I was to visit Lisa in New York.

"Danny, man, I totally underestimated you," said Kierce. "If I'd known you could throw a haymaker like that, I never would have thought you were queer. I guarantee you, after that fight, you'll have girls hanging off you. Rule One Hundred and Six: Girls love a tough guy."

I laughed. "So I'm a tough guy now, huh?" Kierce got so much wrong sometimes that it wasn't even worth arguing with him. He could go on assuming that only straight guys got in fights, and that gay guys never fell for girls. If life was that simple for him, I wasn't going to be able to teach him very much.

"Well, guys," Kierce said, "I'd better get home. My mom will be freaking out about packing. She wants to be on the road super early tomorrow. Gross."

We walked with him to where he'd parked his van.

"You guys want a lift?" he asked.

"Nah, I think I'll go hang out at Jay's place for a while," I said.

"Well, boys, it's been a slice," he said. "I'm gonna miss you guys, in a totally non-gay way."

"Of course," I said.

"Always remember Rule Four: Don't let the bastards grind you down."

He gave us both brief dude hugs and then jumped in his van and pulled away, spinning his tires. He gave a quick honk of his horn before disappearing around the corner.

"What a guy, hey?" asked Jay.

"Yeah."

"This year's gonna be pretty different," he said. "Kierce is gone. You and I won't be in the same grade."

"Different's okay," I said. He nodded.

I was glad I'd come to say goodbye to Kierce. He could be a real dick, and who knows how he'd react if he ever found out that I really was gay, but I knew I'd never meet anyone like him again. You could say a lot of things about the guy, but he never pretended to be anything he wasn't. Maybe that was one thing he'd taught me, even if he'd never actually come out and said it.

"So I've been thinking about seeing if Maisie wants to do something with me," Jay said as we were walking to his place. "You know, like a date, or whatever."

I laughed. "A date? You gonna take her to the Spot?"

"Seriously, man, do you think it's a good idea?"

I thought about it for a minute. "I don't know for sure, but I think you should give it a shot." I hoped she went for it. I had a feeling they'd be good for each other.

We walked along in silence for a few minutes, and then Jay stopped abruptly and turned to me.

"So—are you?" he asked.

"Am I what?" I asked. My heart started pounding furiously in my chest, and I felt my throat go dry.

"You know. Are you—gay?"

I looked at him, and for a few moments I didn't say anything as a million things rushed through my mind at once. I thought about fighting with Kierce, about being enthralled by Lisa, about falling in love with cooking and realizing what I wanted to do with my life. I thought about me and Jay as kids, racing our bikes up and down the hill by his house. I thought about us sneaking beer to the Spot for the first time, and about slowly starting to think about life outside Deep Cove. I thought about all the secrets I'd kept and the lies I'd told to myself and everyone else for so long.

"Yeah," I said finally. "I am."

He thought about that for a moment.

"You know what, Dan? I'm totally cool with that. Way to go, buddy."

I took one look at his big dumb smile and knew without a doubt that he meant it.

TWENTY-FOUR

In Deep Cove, it doesn't take long for summer to dissolve into memory.

September rolls around, the water gets colder by the day, and the wind pushes endless billows of gray and purple clouds across the sky. Heavy frothing waves churn up onto the newly deserted beach, and shorts and flip-flops are replaced with jeans and sweaters. Tourists and summer residents disappear, and town slows down a little as the people who are left behind take a deep breath and prepare to get back to the real world.

I reluctantly traded knives and cutting boards for pencils and paper and got back to the grind, waking up early and catching the school bus, pushing through homework, worrying about grades. Within a few days of school starting up again, it felt like I'd never left.

But I missed the Sandbar. Every math equation I struggled through or short story I analyzed just made me wish I was back in the kitchen, melting chocolate for ganache, or watching JP whip up a new seafood sauce.

Jay had asked Maisie out on a romantic picnic, of all things. I'd gone over to his house and showed him how to make fried chicken. We'd even baked a pie. Now the two of them were officially a couple. They were crazy about each other, and not only had Jay made a major effort to quit smoking, but he'd also allowed Maisie to start tutoring him so he could take a couple of correspondence courses and still graduate with us in June. He had plans to go to the local community college and take a landscaping program.

Being honest about myself with Maisie and Jay made me feel a lot less lonely, and better about life in general. I didn't feel as crazy anymore, and as Maisie put it, if you took Ferris and his buddies seriously, you might as well expect to feel shitty about life. Jay seemed to think that my family would be cool with it when I got around to telling them. I figured he was right, at least about my mom. Dad would need some time to get used to things, but I had a feeling that he'd come around in the same way he had about cooking school. As for Alma, I started to think that having a gay older brother might be one of the best things that ever happened to her.

Mom and Alma were going to come with me to Montreal for my interview at Atwater at the beginning of November. I was pretty excited, but also kind of nervous. I didn't know what I'd do if I didn't make the cut. In the meantime, the three of us were really starting to look forward to the big trip.

"I can't wait to get to Montreal," Alma said. "'This town just ain't big enough for me.'" Dad had planned to come with us, but right after school started, his old boss had called to say that he'd landed a big contract and there was a job waiting for him in Alberta. It sucked that he had to leave again so soon, but I knew my parents were relieved. He'd be gone all fall, and though we hoped he'd be home for Christmas, it was hard to tell with these things.

The day before Dad left, my whole family went for a walk on the beach.

"Man, I hate to leave this place," said Dad as we strolled along the sand. Alma was down on the edge of the waves, trying to skip stones, although the water was too choppy for that.

"At least you know it's always here to come back to," said my mom, taking his arm and leaning into his shoulder.

"You kids don't know how good you have it," he went on. "You have your whole lives to look forward to. Anything could happen."

I remembered Lisa's mom saying almost the same thing. Would I feel that way when I was their age? Was everyone just bound to end up feeling sad about their younger days? It didn't matter. All you could do was roll with it.

Alma ran up and gave me a shove. "Wanna race?" she asked.

"Why not?" I said. "Count of three. One. Two—"

She took off, not waiting for three.

"Hey, no fair!" I yelled, laughing. But I chased her anyway. I caught up and passed her. The wind was pushing against me in big erratic gusts that whipped my hair back and forth across my face and pressed my shirt tight against my chest. I stopped, finally, and turned around. Alma had given up and was walking back to meet my parents. Beyond them I could see Deep Cove, perched on the cliff over the water. It was an image I could have drawn from memory.

I had all the time in the world to be somebody different, somewhere else. For now, the way I saw it, I was right where I was supposed to be.

ACKNOWLEDGMENTS

A huge thank-you to my parents for their love and support, and for choosing to raise their family in the wilds of Cape Breton. Thank you to my brothers—when you're a kid growing up in the country, four minds are so much better than one. Thank you to Frank Macdonald, "the godfather," for setting such a great example. Thank you to my many wonderful friends—their enthusiasm and encouragement is the fuel in my tank. Thank you to the whole gang at the Casual Gourmet, where I learned that I loved food and Nina Simone and that I hated washing dishes. Thank you to Wheeler, the best companion a frustrated writer could ever ask for. Thank you to Robin Stevenson, for her kindness, guidance and lifesaving beer breaks at the Fernwood Inn. Thank you to Deborah Wills, whose words of encouragement are still with me after all these years. Thank you to everyone at Orca, for being so great to work with. Finally, a special thank-you to my editor, Sarah Harvey, for taking a chance on me and for helping me find the story in the middle of all the words.

TOM RYAN was born and raised in Inverness on Cape Breton Island. After high school, he studied English at Mount Allison University and then moved to Halifax, where he studied film production at Nova Scotia Community College. He currently lives in Victoria, British Columbia, with his partner and dog, and dreams of eventually moving home to beautiful Nova Scotia. *Way to Go* is his first novel.

www.tomwrotethat.com